THE MAESTRO'S APPRENTICE

RHONDA LEIGH JONES

ravenous romance™

RED SILK EDITIONS

First published in paperback in 2010 by
Red Silk Editions
500 Third Street, Suite 230
San Francisco, CA 94107

First published as an e-book in 2009 by
Ravenous Romance
100 Cummings Center
Suite 123A
Beverly, MA 01915
www.ravenousromance.com

ISBN: 978-1-59003-209-1

Cover design by April Martinez
Cover photograph © Literary Partners Group, Inc.
Printed in Canada

TCP

10 9 8 7 6 5 4 3 2 1

The paper used in this publication meets the minimum requirements of the American National Standard for Information Sciences—Permanence of Paper for Printed Library Materials Z39.48-1992 (R1997).

Chapter One

AUTUMN COULDN'T help but indulge a sense of impending doom as she crept into the way-too-expensive hotel room in New Orleans' French Quarter, which was sticky with heat even in November. *The place smells funny,* she thought. Part unused and part smoked-in, fucked-in, schemed-in. Worn pink velvet covered the ornate desk chair, faded, as though it had once been red.

It looked like the sort of place a person would hide in, get caught in and get dragged away from. Autumn wondered if she should be bothered by the fact that this made her wet, even though getting caught was the last thing she wanted to have happen. She wasn't *that* much of a masochist.

"Do you think Claudio will find us here?" she asked suddenly.

Claudio du Fresne was the vampire who had been her master, and technically still was. Unless they could stay one step ahead of him.

"Let's hope not," Adam said, unaware that someone else had found them—a man with far more sinister intentions than Claudio.

Adam put his bag and his saxophone on the bed, pulling his long, heavy dreadlocks back once his hands were free. He was a handsome vampire, with medium-toned black skin and a muscular frame. At six feet, he was slightly taller than Claudio. He had been the most relaxed vampire in his maker's chamber quartet, wearing mostly Birkenstock sandals, khaki travel pants and colorful T-shirts advertising his musical, political and spiritual tastes. Today it was bright green and Jimi Hendrix.

He rubbed the dark scruff forming on his chin after being on a bus for most of two days. "If he does find us, our ass is grass. Claudio don't exactly appreciate being robbed. At least we left him his car at the bus station."

"Oh my God," Maria said, rolling her eyes and dropping her bag on the floor. She was bigger, more buxom than the pale, willowy Autumn. She tossed her dark hair aggressively and gestured, turning from one to the other. "What is wrong with you two? This is supposed to be our new life. This is supposed to be exciting, and you have done nothing but worry about what Claudio will do since we left. He doesn't know where we are. And you—" she said, turning to Adam, who had thrown himself on the bed and put both arms over his eyes.

"Damn!" Adam said before she could finish, then jumped up to pace the room. "I just can't believe it's gone. Damned hurricane wiped out every damned thing."

The emotion in his voice made Autumn turn, made her forget Claudio for the moment. Adam was not like most of the other vampires she had met. In her experience, people likely to be turned tended to be exotic in some way—old-world, artistic or just plain eccentric. They craved attention. Adam had played second violin in Claudio's chamber quartet for about sixty years, but he wasn't flashy like the others. He burned incense, wore hemp bracelets and wood necklaces, and kept his hair long.

Autumn put her things by the bed and went to squeeze between him and his saxophone, tugging at her long hippie skirt and putting her arm on his stomach. She felt bad about what she and Maria had decided to do—leave him and go off on their own. It had sounded like a good idea when Maria came up with it. If they were ever going to be free to live their own lives, they would have to break their dependence on the bite. But Autumn had always liked Adam, and now she had second thoughts about everything—leaving Adam, staying with Adam…being with Maria. She looked at the other girl and found Maria looking back at her. She wasn't smiling. Autumn supposed she felt jealous.

Maria had never mentioned jealousy, but back on Claudio's estate, Autumn had felt tension flowing off her whenever one of the vampires came to feed on Autumn or take her sexually. It had always made her feel a little sad for Maria, and a little annoyed at her for making her feel guilty.

Like now.

She closed her eyes and squeezed Adam tighter. "I'm sorry about your mama's house, Adam," she said. "You haven't been here for a long time, have you?"

"Nope," he said, putting his arms around her absently and patting her. "Not since she died back in the sixties. Always meant to, though."

"Well, it's good you get to be here now," Maria said, shoving her shirts and extra pair of jeans into one of the drawers. "You should enjoy it. We plan to. That right, baby?"

Autumn stuffed a bit of light red hair behind her ear as she gave Maria a mischievous look, then lowered her eyes coyly and nodded. Maria smiled. Maria always smiled when Autumn flirted with her, but now Autumn felt a little strange about it. She didn't want to lead her on. Beyond that, she wasn't sure what she *did* want.

"Well," Maria said, scrutinizing a wrinkled T-shirt. "I for one have never been here before and I want to have some fun. Enjoy this freedom we've been talking about for so long, in this land of decadence."

"Oooh, me too!" Autumn said enthusiastically.

Adam shook his head and sat up, dumping Autumn on the mattress. "I can't believe you two. Didn't you get enough decadence with Claudio?"

Maria threw the shirt into the drawer and turned around, gesturing as she talked. "That was *his* decadence. *His* pleasure. His this, his that. His everything. We were just there to give him what he wanted. Now it's our turn to get what we want, Adam. Don't you want that?"

Adam put his hands on his knees and let out a breath, not quite sighing. "Baby girl, I don't even rightly know what I want, and that's the truth. I just know that wasn't it. Too much talk about slaves and punishment and all that craziness. I ain't about no slaves. There are people who want to feed vampires and I'm going to find them. They can come and go as they want. And I'm damned sure not going to beat them."

"Not even for fun?" Autumn asked, forcing herself to sit up and grin. In spite of finding Claudio frightening, something about Adam's declaration made her a little sad.

"Please," he said, standing up. "In my time, I saw enough black folk taken out of their homes and beaten half to death, and I ain't never thought doing that to somebody would be fun. God did not intend us to do that to each other."

Maria took her cue from Autumn and grinned, sauntering over to him. "Haven't you ever wanted to get even, just a little?" She pressed her large breasts against him and ran her hand over his tight abdomen, working her way down to his crotch. It wasn't long before Autumn could see the imprint of his erection through his shorts, and the tips of his fangs between his parted lips.

"You better not start something you ain't prepared to finish," he breathed. "And no, I don't want to get even. My mama did not raise me that way."

Autumn joined Maria and got on her knees in front of him to unbutton his pants with tiny, nimble fingers, thinking about how pretty the three of them were together—Adam's skin the color of lightly creamed coffee, Maria's light, half-Latina coloring and Autumn's translucence.

By the time Autumn got his pants open, Adam's erection was nearly at full mast, with shiny pre-come dripping off the end. She caught it with her tongue and teased the slick head with the tip. "Damn, that feels good," he said.

Adam's erection was too heavy to stand up on its own, so Autumn had to support it with her hand as she played with the thick head, circling it, then stretching her tongue to tease the underside. He groaned. "You got good at that," he breathed.

She smiled up at him and stretched her mouth over the head, changing the rhythm of her breathing to fit the rhythm of her sliding lips, letting the head of his penis touch the back of her throat, and trying to tighten her lips around him.

Maria soon joined her, licking the base of Adam's erection as Autumn took care of the tip. Adam's legs began to shake as they worked. He made little exclamations of pleasure from time to time—"Damn!" being his favorite – but eventually it was too much for him.

"Hold up, hold up," he said, panting. His fangs were extended. "If I don't lie down, I'm going to fall down with what you two are doing."

Autumn pulled back his cock like a lever and ran her tongue along the underside from base to tip, standing as she did. Adam sucked in a big, surprised breath. Then he pulled off his shirt to reveal a well-muscled chest and arms. He wasn't huge by anyone's standards, but it was obvious he visited a weight bench regularly. Tight little black curls dotted his chest and stomach.

He kicked off his shoes and discarded his shorts while Autumn and Maria pulled their shirts over their heads and unhooked each other's bras. Maria moved Autumn's straps down her arms, pressing her own bare breasts against the other girl's back, and reached around to cup her breasts, teasing the nipples while Autumn slid the bra to the ground.

Autumn closed her eyes. It was such a nice moment, and she wished difficult conversations weren't looming over them. She wished they could all just enjoy each other's company without expectations.

"Hey," Adam said. "Y'all started something big, now come over here and finish it before you drive me crazy."

The two looked over at him, sprawled on the bed with a meaty erection flopped over his leg. Autumn giggled and started to go over to him. Maria hugged her tight for one more moment before letting go. Autumn paused at the edge of the bed to get out of her sandals and hippie skirt before pressing her small, pale frame to his large, dark one, kissing his full lips.

His tight pubic curls felt good against her shaved crotch, so she rubbed herself back and forth over them as she buried her fingers in his dreads and put her tongue in his mouth. His hands went to her back, running up and down as he responded eagerly to her kiss.

Behind her, Maria followed his hands with kisses, making Autumn shiver. She enjoyed it, but it reminded her of the reason she had to break up with Maria. With all their talk of freedom, Maria was constantly trying to rein her in, draw Autumn's attention to herself.

Autumn wanted to put freedom to the test.

She had no idea what she would do if Adam moved to bite her. Unlike movie vampires, real ones didn't kill their food. Usually, they kept people as chattel to be fed on and fucked. Vampire bodily fluids contained chemicals that altered the bodies of feeders in wonderful ways, slowing down the aging process, making them impervious to disease and helping injuries heal quickly. But it also made them crave the vampire or vampires who fed on them. With some, the bite became an addiction. Autumn's body cried out for it even now, and trembled with anticipation.

Maria pressed her naked form against Autumn's and kissed her shoulder. "My darling," she whispered as Autumn humped Adam's writhing body. Adam pulled his hands from between the two and squeezed Autumn's thigh. She pictured his other hand touching Maria. For some reason that drove her into a frenzy, made her move against him frantically, her tongue doing a dangerous dance around his extended fangs, tempting her to pierce her own flesh so he would feed. Behind her, Maria moaned. Adam jerked his head to the side.

"I'm going to roll over," he said.

Maria climbed off so he could roll on top of Autumn, careful not to press too much of his weight on top of her slim frame. His hair haloed his head and eclipsed the overhead light. He grinned. "You sure are something," he said. "Little minx."

She grinned. Maria stretched out beside them and played with Autumn's long red hair, stroking her face with her fingertips. Adam turned to her. "And you ain't much better. I believe the two of you are trying to kill me."

He moved his hips against Autumn's raging pussy, pressing the hard base of the shaft against her swollen labia, causing her to whimper with the sensation of pleasure-pain, while leaning forward to kiss Maria. Autumn watched them smile at each other while Adam humped her. She lifted her legs and wound them around his hips, rutting against him, wishing he would just put it in her. She wished he would bite her.

The kiss between Adam and Maria became more insistent as she ran her hand over his chest and down his stomach, then back again, touching Autumn at the same time. He put his arm around her and pulled her closer. "Get on your back for me," he said, so Maria lay next to Autumn and looked at her. Autumn met her eyes. She knew Maria well enough to guess what she was thinking: *Look what we're doing with Adam.*

Maria always made a unit of herself and Autumn, while Autumn preferred to think of herself as part of the whole, or as one unit with many others who interacted randomly.

Randomness turned her on. That was a good thing, because Adam's cock was pretty hefty. He raised his hips off Autumn and took it in his hand, rubbing the slick head over her opening. It slid easily. "Somebody is ready for it," he teased. "I don't think I've seen you like this before."

She grinned at him, enjoying his large form on top of her, the heat from his body, and his earthy smell. They had been on a bus all day and hadn't showered since sometime yesterday, so Adam had worked up a strong, pleasant musk.

He began to press at her just a little bit. Her lips opened and her lids became heavy with desire. Maria reached over and put her hand between Autumn's legs, teasing her clit while Adam tested her pussy. Autumn gave a little moan, willing all thoughts to leave her head, focusing on nothing but sensation and her feelings for the two people with her.

It was always a shock when Adam entered her, no matter how wet she was. It always felt as though the huge head of his erection had stretched her as far as she could be stretched. But the shaft was even thicker, and stretched her far beyond that, opening her up and fitting into her body as if it were a sleeve designed especially for him. It hurt.

And it felt so incredibly good.

She opened her mouth and let out air like a dying animal while he slid halfway in, to where his cock thickened, and then pulled back slowly. He would have to push it the rest of the way, coax her body to take it, but he liked to tease her first. She liked it too.

Between Adam's giant cock impaling her and Maria's fingers teasing her clit, Autumn was in danger of climaxing too soon, before need had built enough to make the orgasm strong, so she looked up at Adam's face, lips open and fangs erect, tense but at peace. The sight of his fangs made her tingle. What if she stopped taking the bite after just this one time? She could work up to telling him the bad news, instead of springing it on him all at once and ruining such a beautiful moment. Autumn reached up and took a rope of hair in her hand and played with it, distracting herself.

Maria followed suit and touched his hair. He turned to her and smiled, then reached over and put his hand on her breast. "Mm…this is so nice. I'm loving this," he said.

After fucking Autumn with only half the length of his cock for a while, he planted his elbows on either side of her and lowered his head, covering her with his hair. "Ready for the rest, baby girl?" he asked.

She nodded. He slid it in until it stopped and began pushing it, giving tiny thrusts of his hips to tease his way in. Autumn gave an open-mouthed gasp as he stretched her further. The pain intensified the pleasure. "Oh my God, Adam," she whispered.

"You're gonna take it," he said, giving a harder thrust, forcing his way in more. "I'm gonna fuck you good." His voice was a low, husky growl. His body shook. Autumn knew it was because of the control he was exerting over his own excitement, that he really just wanted to pound her until he came. That would happen later. For now, he had to concentrate on filling her up completely.

His dreads tented around her as he lowered his head to kiss her on the lips, then moved to her jaw and down to her neck. A jolt of adrenaline surged through her. Maria's fingers left Autumn's pussy and squeezed her thigh in short, quick bursts. Autumn knew Maria was trying to signal her to tell Adam not to bite her, but Autumn ignored her. She was now desperate for the bite, and exposed her throat for him.

"Adam…" Maria said urgently, but he didn't respond. He kissed the spot over Autumn's jugular. "Adam," she said louder. "Don't bite us…okay?"

Autumn wanted to scream, but she didn't dare. She had agreed to leave with Maria. They had talked about it for so long. But her body felt as though it would explode if Adam didn't penetrate her in every way possible this minute.

He paused, dragged himself away from the kiss and whispered, "What?"

Autumn looked up. It was on the tip of her tongue to tell Maria to stop interfering. But she didn't do that. She accepted what Maria wanted, like she always did.

"Please," Maria said. "I'll explain later."

Looking as though he was about to throw up, Adam nodded and pressed his cheek against Autumn's before pushing into her with the thick base of his cock. Disappointment about the bite dampened her enthusiasm, but she raised her hips to meet him. He pulled out a couple of inches and pushed it back in. She could feel him deep inside her.

Maria relaxed her hold on Autumn's thigh, then began kneading the sensitive flesh as the pair rutted against each other. Autumn had forgotten Maria was even touching her, and wished she would stop. She held Adam tighter and turned her thoughts to him as he fucked her hard. His need brought back her excitement. She felt lightheaded. Her legs shook and her calf threatened to cramp because of the way she tensed when she was close. She ignored it and climaxed with a surprised cry. That was all it took to take Adam over the edge. Autumn groaned as she felt his cock throbbing against her sensitive walls and his hot juices filling her.

She still wanted him to bite her, but at least she felt much more relaxed now. Autumn sighed, wondering what it said about her that she felt so annoyed with Maria right now. She felt guilty.

Adam dropped his head, tickling her face with his hair. Maria moved around so she could curl her body around their heads and pet Autumn's face. Autumn closed her eyes and felt her anger dissipate as she concentrated on the sensations—Maria's feathery fingers, Adam's weight and breathing, the strange feeling of him shrinking inside her.

After a while, Adam raised up on his elbows and looked at her. "I don't know what you're on, but you need to keep taking it. That was…mm!" He shook his head and got up to clean himself.

Autumn looked at Maria to find the other girl staring at her. She tried to recall the feelings she had had for her six months ago when everything had seemed so exciting, and decided they were still there, buried. They had to be. She couldn't just abandon Maria.

"Sorry Maria," Adam said, making his way toward the bathroom. "The next one's yours. I promise. I just wasn't… girl, what has gotten into you?" he asked Autumn.

"Adam, we have to talk to you," Maria said.

"I'm listening," he said, returning with a towel. He stood in the middle of the room milking excess come from his cock. "And what's up with not wanting to be bitten? I'm starting to get hungry."

The girls shared a look. "Uh-oh. You two are cooking something up. What is it?"

Maria took Autumn's hand. Autumn let her, curious to see how it made her feel. She felt detached.

"We want to strike out on our own," Maria said. "Get out of the whole vampire thing."

The jovial look on Adam's face disappeared. "Oh. I see," he said. "Well, then. How long? When?"

"Not right away, Adam," Autumn said quickly, pulling her hand away from Maria's and sitting up. "I mean, if you can't find food, of course we'll feed you..."

"You'll find food," Maria said. "We'll help you. And we'll stay with you a few weeks, or until you have somebody permanent."

"And we can keep doing this," Autumn added.

Adam nodded and tossed the towel on the bed. "Yeah."

"Are you okay?" Autumn asked, going to him.

He backed away a step and put his hand up reflexively, then moved it to the back of his neck. "Yeah, I'm fine. I'm going to go take a shower. Y'all figure out where you want to go."

Autumn stopped, stung by his withdrawal. "Want company?" she asked hopefully.

"No, baby girl. I've got it. You and Maria talk about what you want to do tonight."

Autumn thought he sounded hurt. She watched him go, wishing such a wonderful time hadn't ended like this, feeling guilty and trying to convince herself she still felt the same about Maria. Her heart beat too quickly. The bathroom door shut. Autumn told herself this would all work out.

"Hey," Maria said from the bed. "Why don't we take Adam to a strip club tonight?"

Chapter Two

WATCHED BY patient, unseen eyes, they wound up at a two-level club on Bourbon Street where a beautiful brunette dancer in red inched her way to the top of the pole, which extended from the floor on the first level to the ceiling on the second, where Autumn and the others had gone. The upper level was essentially a three hundred and sixty-degree loft from which people could watch the goings-on below. Autumn watched as the girl wrapped her slender legs around it, undulating as though she were making love. Autumn imagined the cold metal pressed against her own crotch while dozens of men, watched and wanted.

She hardly noticed how sulky Adam had become.

"Why don't I just get a drink and go out on the balcony?" he suggested, unaware it was being staked out by a man in the shadows across the street.

Autumn watched the pole.

"I think she wants to see the show, Adam," Maria teased.

"She can do what she wants. I'm going outside."

Autumn whirled around. The multicolored lights, thumping music and scantily clad bodies made her feel giddy. "Oh, come on!" she said, circling her arms around one of his, squeezing his large, round bicep because she liked the vein running along the side. "Have some fun with us! Just this one night, can we please just pretend we don't have to worry so much? Please?"

Adam wrinkled the side of his mouth and sighed, giving her a look. He was so handsome with his top dreads pulled back. "All right, all right. If you really want me to let some girl shake her coochie in my face…"

Before he could finish, however, a girl with a silvery-blonde pixie cut and glitter on her temples approached them with a smile. "My name's Tina," she said to Maria, before giving Autumn a warm smile. "Is this your first time here?"

"Yes," Autumn said, excited. "Are you one of the dancers?"

"I am," Tina said. "Can I interest you girls or your friend here in a lap dance?"

"Oooh, that would be so much fun," Maria said, putting one hand on Adam's shoulder and one on his arm. "This is Adam, and he really needs to have a good time."

"No, he doesn't," Adam said. "It was y'all's crazy notion to come in here. I just want a drink."

Autumn and Maria both looked at him, alarmed. He looked from one to the other. "Of *Jack*. As in Jack and Coke."

"If Adam gets one, can we watch?" Autumn asked.

"No," Adam said. "Because I am not getting one."

"Of course," Tina said. "It'll cost ten dollars more each, but you'll be fucking like bunnies later, I guarantee it."

Adam shifted his weight to another foot and looked away with a sigh. "I do not believe this," he mumbled. "Can't take you two anywhere."

"Oh, come on," Autumn said, popping him lightly on the butt. "We just want you to have fun."

"Out of guilt. I know what you're doing. This is not going to help matters any, I'll tell you that."

Autumn's smile wilted. Tears stung her eyes, but no one saw. She was glad.

"Follow me," Tina said, and walked toward a corridor parallel to the stairwell.

"Get him," Maria told Autumn, then took his left hand in hers and followed Tina. Autumn ignored the hurt and guilt she felt about Maria telling Adam they were leaving him, and made herself grab his other hand to help pull him along. Adam shook his head and allowed himself to be led to a tiny room with a bench on one end that looked like a shelf, and a mirror on the other that covered all but about six inches of the wall.

Maria pulled Autumn out of the way as the pixie-haired stripper motioned to Adam to sit on the bench and stood in the middle of the room. "You guys must be really close," she said over her shoulder to the girls, just as Maria pulled Autumn to her and nuzzled her hair. Then Tina grinned. "Really, *really* close."

"Yeah," Maria said, gazing at Autumn affectionately. Autumn smiled, and ignored the discomfort it caused, and the fact that she really didn't want Maria to touch her right now.

I wonder if I really don't want to be with her, she wondered, before pushing the thought away. The prospect of being free to float wherever the wind decided to take her gave her butterflies.

Autumn had always been subject to the whims of others, and had never really done much. Except for being bounced around from one foster home to another during her teens, she had led an extremely sheltered life before meeting Claudio five years before, at the age of twenty. At first, life at the vampire's estate had seemed exciting, with parties, constant sex and the persistent, looming threat of punishment.

But before long, a certain sameness had set in. Though she'd had some interesting experiences at Claudio's place, she hadn't had the freedom to experiment—not that she'd wanted to then. Claudio was a very sexy Frenchman, and she had come to love him. But he would punish his feeders with a belt or a riding crop in a heartbeat, plus he enjoyed frightening, kinky games. She'd thought she would get used to him eventually, but he scared her as much now as he had when she'd first met him. Maria's plan to run had been a way to escape the fear and experience a new way of living.

Out here, she wasn't scared anymore. The excitement of the open road and all of Maria's talk about doing what they wanted had gotten Autumn questioning what she wanted. The answer that came back to her was one simple word.

Everything.

Adam leaned against the wall and put his hands on his thighs. Tina began to gyrate her hips while pulling her top over her head, exposing her lean back to the girls. Adam's eyebrows shot up. He cleared his throat. "Do you like it?" she asked, and turned around to wiggle her butt at him while she opened her shorts, winking at the girls.

"Oh yeah," Adam said. "It's nice."

Autumn began to feel the deep heat between her legs spread upward to her belly, while her thighs tingled, giving her a pleasant, hot-and-cold sensation. Maria began fingering a nipple. Watching a strange girl wiggle barely two feet away while the four of them huddled in the tiny back room of a New Orleans strip bar was intoxicating.

Tina bent over and took her shorts on a slow ride down her legs. Autumn watched Adam's look of appreciation as he stared at her naked ass. One corner of his mouth lifted in a smile. "Now, that's nice," he said.

For a moment, Autumn wanted to be like her.

Tina wiggled her thong at Adam a little more before stepping out of her shorts, snagging her see-through heels on them briefly. While unhooking the shorts from the shoe, she looked up at the girls. "Do you want to join him on the bench?"

Autumn opened her mouth to say yes, but felt Maria's hand tense around her waist. "No, we're fine," Autumn said. "This is all for Adam."

"You don't know what you're missing," Tina sing-songed. She winked at Autumn, whose butterflies danced. She was up for anything, and that would scare her if she wasn't with the two people she trusted most in the world.

Tina moved close to Adam. "How are you doing?"

"I'm doing fine," he said. He held his mouth funny, so Autumn figured his fangs were just as erect as his cock, which bulged against the leg of his jeans. He shifted to make it easier for Tina to straddle his thighs, and rested his hands on the bench at his sides.

"You must be," she said, making a show of checking out his package. "So you *can* relax after all."

"I'm relaxed," he said. "But my girls here want to spend all my money on the first night."

"Your girls?" she said, squeezing her pale, round breasts and rubbing her inner thighs on his outer thighs as she gyrated. "Are you three together?"

"Something like that," he said. "It's complicated."

"It always is," Tina said with a laugh. "You can touch me if you want." She put her hands on his shoulders and lowered herself until her barely covered pussy almost brushed his thighs as she moved. Adam put his hands on her hips.

Autumn thought the contrast of his dark fingers against her pale skin was pretty. She didn't get to look for long though, because Maria began kissing her cheek, moving on a diagonal path to the corner of her mouth, teasing with the tip of her tongue.

Autumn thought she would die if she didn't get fucked soon and fucked hard. Her breath came out ragged as Maria got between her and the spectacle on the bench and pressed her into the corner, covering her lips and invading her mouth with a frantic tongue.

Girls are soft kissers, Autumn thought. *Too soft.* She closed her eyes and imagined the length of Adam's swollen cock the way it had been a few hours before, insistently burrowing its way into her. The thought made her press against Maria and draw her close, devouring kisses as a part of her mind made a note that she really wasn't into it that much, and would have to make a decision sooner or later. She had no idea how long it was before Tina exclaimed, "Oh my God! Are those *fangs*?"

Chapter Three

MARIA AND Autumn froze.

"They *are* fangs, aren't they?" Tina said.

Maria turned the top half of her body to see what was going on while Autumn just stood against the wall with her mouth open. Adam, along with every other vampire they had ever met, had been so careful about keeping his fangs hidden, even when they grew, that they had simply not foreseen him getting careless in a strip club, of all places. It wasn't as though Adam didn't have access to beautiful women.

Tina stood with Adam's thighs between her legs. He clamped his mouth shut, and sat with his arms in midair and a wary expression, watching her. Tina dismounted him awkwardly and stood holding her arms away from her body, also poised, looking at him. She bent forward slightly. Then she took a step toward him and said something no one in the room expected.

"Can I see?"

Adam moved his head back, as though he'd just discovered she had something contagious. "What?" he asked.

"Can I see? Your fangs. I want to see them."

"There ain't no fangs," he said, and got up, scowling and adjusting his cock inside his pants.

"I saw them," she insisted. "Look, I'm from here, okay? I've seen some pretty weird things and I know what I saw. You had fangs two minutes ago that you didn't have when you came in here. Are you a vampire?"

"Come on," Adam said to the girls. "Let's go."

They crowded with him at the door.

"I want you to bite me," Tina said.

He stopped with his hand on the doorknob. "I ain't no vampire," he said unconvincingly.

"But only if you can do it without killing me," Tina added. "I'm not suicidal."

He turned around. Tina looked at the girls with an expression of open urgency. "Are you vampires too?"

They shook their heads, too stunned to speak.

Tina looked at Adam. "Please? Life here is so shallow. It's stimulating and…thrilling, in its own way, but you build up a tolerance. I just want to feel something."

Autumn knew exactly what she meant.

Tina stepped forward and put her hand over Adam's heart. "I want to give you what you need. Just for a little while. If it's okay."

"It's okay with us," Maria said, assuming Autumn's agreement, as usual. This time, she was right.

Adam flashed a look at them, then nodded and shifted on his feet. "All right," he said. "But we leave right now. And you don't tell anybody."

She nodded, and began a hasty re-dress. "A couple of the girls here tonight owe me. I can get them to cover."

She took them to the bar, told the bartender to give them three drinks on her ticket. "Wait for me," she said emphatically and headed across the room.

"What do you want?" the bartender asked.

Adam shook his head and leaned on the bar, dropping down hard between his shoulders. "Jack and Coke," he said.

"I'll have a Corona," Maria said. "She doesn't drink."

"I'll have a Cosmopolitan," Autumn chimed in.

Maria widened her eyes. "You don't drink," she insisted.

"Well, tonight I do," Autumn said.

In spite of telling Adam they were leaving, and in spite of the imminent breakup with Maria, Autumn felt deliciously wicked—in New Orleans, picking up a stripper *and* drinking a Cosmopolitan. She would liked to have stayed out a while longer, but wanted to see what happened with Adam and Tina. Not to mention she was glad he had found a meal.

He was right, though. She did feel guilty. But there was something more, too. Something about leaving him just felt wrong.

It wasn't long before Tina had made arrangements to have the rest of her shift covered and changed into street clothes. She was a tiny, waifish thing in tiny, waifish jeans, a metal-studded belt and tight, neon-pink-on-white T-shirt. "Ready?" she asked.

Adam had finished his drink almost as soon as it had been served. Maria wasn't really interested in her beer, and Autumn was only about halfway through with hers. She didn't want to let it go, so she downed the rest. "Oooh," she said, climbing off the barstool. The floor felt a little unsteady.

"Careful," Tina said, and put her hand on Autumn's arm.

Maria watched the exchange closely.

"Thanks," Autumn said.

Their hotel was only a few minutes' walk away. Tina chattered about different bars and told them where the nearest Internet café was, while Autumn pointed out things she thought were pretty, like the guy with closely cropped hair and tight jeans who had just crossed their path. Tina giggled. Maria grew quiet, and Adam put his arm around her.

Back in the room, Tina looked at Adam with bright, open eyes. She hooked her thumbs in her pockets and twisted her body back and forth. "I've been doing this a couple of years and you're the first vampire I've met."

"You sound like you expected to meet some."

She shrugged and sat on one of the beds. "You hear things, especially here. You just never know what's true." She glanced at the girls. "So what's the…what do I do?"

Adam sat beside her, leaned over and kissed her.

"Whoa," she said, pulling away to look at him. "They're out again."

"They do that when I'm hungry," he said. "Or turned on."

"So which is it?" she asked.

"Both," he said, and pulled her back onto the mattress. Autumn watched as he put his hand up the other girl's shirt. She was turned on.

Maria rubbed Autumn's arm. "Come on," she whispered, and pulled her toward the bed. Autumn let Maria pull her shirt over her head and take off her bra, then position her on the mattress and tease her breasts with her tongue while Tina whispered to Adam on the other bed.

"I want you to fuck me," Tina whispered.

Autumn strained to hear everything going on in the other bed as Maria tried to get her attention. She smiled up at Maria and kissed her back, but closed her eyes and pretended she was the one who had happened to find a strange vampire in a strip bar as she raised her hips so Maria could pull off her jeans. While Maria unfolded her labia with her tongue and ran the tip along the delicate inside, Autumn pretended she was the one in a den of strangers, and that she had never seen Maria before, never been with a girl before. She pretended everything was new.

"Fuck me, Adam," Tina whined. "Your cock is so huge. Do all vampires have such massive cocks?"

"Nope," Adam said.

When the bed creaked, Autumn turned her head and opened her eyes, thrusting her pussy against Maria's searching tongue. Adam was on his feet, pulling off the girl's clothes and his own. Then he covered Tina's waifish frame with his nude body and worked his way into her. "Oh God," she said. "I want you to fuck me."

It wasn't long before Adam was pumping his hips against Tina's naked pussy and she was moving against him, arms wrapped around his neck and pulling him close to her. Autumn wondered if it was impolite to watch a strange person having sex with someone she knew, but the sight of them and the sounds of Adam's grunting and Tina's mewling drove her too hard.

He was a lot more animalistic with Tina than he ever was with her, growling deep in his throat, thrusting almost violently. Autumn envied her that, even though she was glad Adam always took care of her. Tina was probably a lot more experienced, she thought, and that's why she got to have wild, abandoned sex without having to consider the consequences.

Autumn was desperate for pleasure without consequence.

She watched as something passed between Adam and Tina. He slowed his thrusting and looked into her eyes. She gazed back into his and swallowed. Then Adam lowered his head and began to nuzzle her neck, still rocking his hips. Finally, Autumn saw him open his mouth and lift his lip over his fangs like a snarling dog. Tina's whole body convulsed as he pierced her. She gave a squeal and held him tight as he drew hungry gulps from the wounds he had made, while Maria worked between Autumn's legs.

Adam drank for a long time, which was unusual for a first bite. It made Autumn feel a little guilty, because she figured it meant he was hungrier than he'd been letting on. She had often heard that "virgin blood"—or blood from someone who had never been bitten before—tasted unripe.

Tina's movements calmed, then stopped, as Adam continued to ravish her, working his whole body back and forth as he drank. Finally he tore himself away, took a deep breath and groaned in climax. There was a dribble of blood on his bottom lip and another on her neck.

Autumn gave Maria obligatory hip-thrusts as she watched them, feeling disconnected from her girlfriend's moans of pleasure. She was glad Maria tended to close her eyes while going down.

Adam settled back down on Tina and looked at her face. "You okay?" he asked softly.

She turned her face to him slowly, like someone who had been drugged. "You have some on your lip," she said, and giggled.

He wiped it off with his thumb and stuck it in his mouth, then made a face. "It's better while it's warm," he said. "Hold still," he said, then lowered his head and lapped up the blood from her neck. "Did you like it?" he asked.

She nodded groggily.

"Just so you know, a vampire can't get or give STDs and we can't father crumb-snatchers. So you're safe. You're going to want to sleep for a while."

"How long?"

"Day, day and a half. It depends. But you're going to feel pretty damned good when you wake up. And hungry."

She nodded again, then didn't move. Autumn closed her eyes while Maria touched and licked her. Adam got up, cleaned himself and Tina, then put her under the covers.

Autumn zoned out, enjoying Maria's warm, wet tongue, surprised to find Adam sitting on the other bed and watching them when she opened her eyes. He was hard again, and stroking the length of his cock as he watched, propping on one straight arm so that the side head of his triceps bulged. His head lolled back. His dreads looked like a mane.

Autumn watched his fingers spread the slick pre-come around the thick head, then work it down the shaft with his whole hand. He got up and gave them a smoky look before getting on his knees behind Maria and reaching around to open her jeans. He pulled them just below her ass cheeks and reached between her legs to rub his fingers against her clit and labia. Maria moaned against Autumn, whimpering as Adam began to push his cock into her.

Adam took her fiercely, gripping her hips and slamming her back on his cock, causing her face to rock against Autumn's pussy and vibrate her with groans. The unexpectedness of it all sent Autumn over the edge, although she had to finish herself with her fingers, because Maria was no longer able to concentrate. She lowered her head. Autumn fingered herself among the dark strands of Maria's hair. Then she lay there and felt the motion of their lovemaking, until Adam turned Maria over on her back and fucked her until she whimpered. Eventually, her body shuddered and Adam slowed his thrusting, watching her with a little smile on his lips.

She and Maria showered together sleepily, enjoying affectionate touches and scrubbing each other's backs. Then they climbed into bed, with Maria spooning Autumn while Autumn watched the girl sleeping next to Adam, wondering what her life must be like, if it was more exciting than Autumn's. If she was putting off any unpleasant conversations.

Tomorrow, she promised herself. She would talk to Maria tomorrow.

Chapter Four

AUTUMN WAS awakened by the sounds of someone whispering, "Shit!" Then there were shuffling sounds, and she opened her eyes.

Tina was trying to get her jeans on while standing up, nearly falling over as if she were drunk. Autumn knew it was a side effect of the bite and of getting up too early when they hadn't gotten to bed until the wee hours. It was amazing Tina was up at all. The clock said 12:15. They had been sleeping for only six hours.

Adam snorted and rolled over.

Autumn got out of bed carefully. Tina impaled her with a startled gaze, freezing with one leg mostly in her jeans. "I was trying not to wake anyone up," she whispered. Her mascara was smudged. She scratched at two marks on her neck that looked like picked-at mosquito bites.

Autumn shrugged. "I'm a light sleeper. You should rest more after…"

"My apartment isn't far from here," Tina said. "Besides, I'm used to this kind of thing. Not being bitten by vampires, obviously, but partying late and then making a hasty getaway. It's the price of fun in this town. You guys here long?"

Autumn shook her head. "I don't know. Adam's from here and hasn't been back for a while." She looked over her shoulder as Maria whimpered in her sleep, then turned back to Tina. She had an idea, and it made her heart beat fast. "Do you know of a place I can get takeout?"

Tina shook her head. "Not nearby. Not officially, anyway. But I do know someone who might have a little something left over. I'll show you if you want."

Autumn dressed hurriedly, left a note and grabbed her little pack. Striking out on her own in New Orleans. She loved it. Outside, she took a deep breath of the crisp fall air, ignoring the street smells of too much partying and too little garbage pickup, unaware of the slick stranger keeping pace with them.

"You see the city waking up in layers," Tina said. "The only people out now are like these guys," she said, pointing out an overweight middle-aged couple in polo shirts and shorts, with two pre-teens. They stopped to gaze into a shop window. "They'll take home T-shirts that say, 'I survived NOLA' and cheesy little things to put on their mantle, to prove they were here. The nightlife crowd is still sleeping it off. It's like two different cities, but I guess they all are."

"Have you been anywhere else?"

Tina nodded, then shrugged. "Yeah. No. I don't know. I'm from Lafayette. I was here for school. But I've been here six years now, and it feels like home. City just sucks you in."

"How old are you?" Autumn asked.

"Twenty-four. You?"

"Twenty-five. Maria's thirty, though."

"Wow. She doesn't look it."

"It's a side effect of being a feeder. You hardly age. And people live a long time. Not as long as a vampire, but…

You should come with us. Adam needs another feeder and you're fun."

Tina shook her head. "No can do. I'm dug in here, you know? My friends are here. I'm part of something. But you, I can see you're in breakaway mode."

The comment startled Autumn. She wondered if Maria could tell, or if she would read it as an effect of "their" plan. "How can you tell?"

Tina shrugged. "Just a hunch. I tell you what, though. You have to be careful. People are not always what they seem. That sounds cheesy, but it's true. You have to learn to hear what they're really saying, not what they want you to hear. That's my advice to you if you're going to be sneaking away from your friends in New Orleans. Here we are."

They turned a corner and Tina knocked on a metal service door. "Hey, Luis, open up in there! I need a favor!"

The door opened and a dark-skinned Creole wearing an apron appeared. He looked to be in his late twenties. He smiled when he saw Tina, but his dark eyes flicked curiously over Autumn, making her self-conscious. She wondered what he would be like if they met in a random back alley. Then she had to shake her head to get the thought out of it.

"Hey, Tina. Where you been? You don't like my cooking no more?" His French accent sent a shiver up Autumn's spine and for a moment she remembered to be afraid of Claudio finding them.

"Sure I do, Luis," Tina said. "It's your breath that scares me."

He slapped a hand over his heart. "I'm hurt. I really am. So what kind of favor you need?" He stared at Autumn now.

"I have some friends in town and they are in need of takeout. They're good people, Luis."

He threw his hand up. "Good people, good people. I'm good people, and nobody rains treasures down on my head. Now let's see...not much here that's still good, except biscuits." He squinted at her neck. "Something bite you, *cherie*?"

Tina gave Autumn a horrified look. Autumn shook her head to signal it was okay. "Yeah," she said. "Looks like a couple of mosquitoes got into the room last night." Tina reached up and clasped her hand around her neck. "Big ones," she said.

"Even this time of year." Luis shook his head. "Something always trying to eat you in this town." He looked at Tina. "You look like you're falling down, my love. Go home and rest. Come see me later. I'll take care of your pretty friend."

Tina yawned and nodded. "Sounds like a good idea." To Autumn, she said, "Watch out for this guy. He tries to be smooth."

He flipped a dish towel and caught her on the ass. "Get out of here. You're bad for my game." His smile disappeared as he put some biscuits in a plastic bag. "How many of you are there?"

"Th...two," Autumn said. "Just the two of us. I really appreciate this. We forgot to bring something to our room last night and she's not in any condition to go out to lunch."

"I understand, I understand. Here is some jam for you...and some cheese. This ain't left over, but it's better than just biscuit, no? Tina, she's my friend. So...I take care of her friend." He held out the bag. Autumn reached for it. He pulled it back. "No. First you have to tell me...what is your story?"

"My story?"

"Why not? Everyone has a story. Especially people who come to this place. Tina doesn't roll with people she doesn't think are interesting. So. What makes you interesting?"

Autumn dropped her gaze to the floor under his scrutiny, suddenly very aware she was alone with this strange man, who was eyeing her almost aggressively. "We're just traveling," she said. Then she thought, *why not tell him at least part of it?* She sighed. "Okay, I'll tell you. But you can't tell anyone else. I'm with a girl. I mean, she's my girlfriend. But I really like guys, and I really just want to spend my time in New Orleans having a good time. So I went for a walk to see what I could get into."

"Is that so?" he asked. "What sort of trouble you looking for?"

Autumn shrugged. "I don't know. I guess I'll know it when I see it. Where's a good place to go for a drink this time of day?"

"You really are serious. Out for a good time, eh? Too bad I'm such a nice guy. I could show you some things." He handed her a plastic bundle, which she put into her pack, and told her how to find Lafitte's Blacksmith's Shop at the end of Bourbon Street.

"Be careful, lovely lady," he teased. "It's still haunted by the ghost of the mad pirate Jean Lafitte. In fact, it's his bar."

She wasn't prepared to find herself in an ancient, pitch-black building. The only electric light she could see was over the bar. There was a television with the sound on low. A few men sat at the bar, chatting with a strung-out-looking bartender. He met her eyes immediately. "Yes?" he said.

"Can I have a, uh…drink?" she asked.

"What'll it be?"

"Get the lady a shot of Chartreuse," said a gravelly voice behind her, making her jump. It belonged to a good-looking guy with a face that wasn't exactly chiseled, or weathered. It was a good, solid face that wasn't too pretty and wasn't too worn, but looked like it had seen a thing or two. His brown hair was collar-length in back and receded in front. He held his mouth in a stern expression.

"A shot?" she said, shaking her head. "Oh no, that's too small."

The man smiled and lit a cigarette. Everyone turned to watch the flame light up the room. He thrashed it out and tossed the dead match on the floor.

"Too small, huh?" he said with a smile. His eyes crinkled pleasantly. He looked to be in his forties, and was wearing a gray striped suit with black button-down shirt, no tie. "Make that a double. And I'll take a Smithwick's."

He came up and stood next to Autumn. "I didn't think anybody drank before breakfast other than musicians who'd been up all night."

"You're a musician?" She looked him over, imagining he had followed her into the bar with evil intent, shivering with pleasure.

He nodded. "I've played most of the bars here. Sometimes we just don't make it to bed. Then we crash a day or two later."

"What do you play?"

"Rhythm guitar. That means…I know a thing or two about rhythm, and all the many uses for it." He winked.

"Here you go, Bill," the bartender said, and handed him both glasses—a large one filled with a dark, frothy beer and a small one partially filled with a green liquid.

"Come on," he said with a glass in each hand and cigarette loose between his lips. He motioned with his head, then led Autumn toward the back. Autumn looked around nervously for a moment, then followed him because she didn't want to stand there looking like a dork while some guy made off with the drink he'd just bought her.

This was already turning out to be a strange day. But she'd wanted that.

They sat on a bench at a round table in the back next to the restroom corridor. He dragged the ashtray toward himself and squinted his eyes as he let out the smoke from his last drag.

"You'll like this," he said, nudging the glass toward her. "It tastes like anise. You wouldn't have shot it anyway. It's for savoring, not throwing back." He nodded toward it. "Go ahead."

The candle on the table—there was a candle on every table in the place and it was midday—made him look like a painting, with warm colors fading quickly into the surrounding black. He had an ease about him she found attractive, and dangerous. She picked up the glass and sniffed it, then took a sip. It was strong and spicy. It made her blink fast.

Bill took a sip of his beer. "What do you think?"

"It's good," Autumn said. "What's it called again?"

"Chartreuse."

"It sounds French."

"It is. Brewed by monks. So what's your name, and why are you out accepting drinks from strange men in the middle of the day?"

She looked down, feeling more shy than usual. "This is my first time here, and I just wanted to see things, I guess." She wasn't about to say anything about breaking up or wanting adventure, not to this man. He reminded her of Claudio. Not his general vibe, but the assured calm. Plus, he was a musician who knew about French spirits. The similarity was enough to raise the hairs along her spine, and intrigue her.

He nodded. "What's your name?"

"Autumn," she said hesitantly.

"Pretty. I'm Bill." He held out his hand. For a moment, his intent didn't register, and she just stared at it. Then she took it. It was large, with long, graceful fingers. He squeezed hers, held it for about a second longer than necessary, while keeping his eyes on hers, then let go. "I know all these guys. Play in all these bars. A bunch of us do. It's great. You here alone?"

"No," she said. "I have a couple of friends. They just didn't come out with me. They're sleeping."

"I've noticed something about people who come to New Orleans. They're either after trinkets, or they're looking for something deeper. Something darker. You know what I mean?"

Autumn nodded, although she really didn't have a clue what he was talking about. She found his gravelly voice mesmerizing.

"You don't look like the trinket type, Autumn. It's your season, isn't it? Autumn. That's nice. Autumn came to me in a bar in New Orleans, on the darkest end of Bourbon Street, wearing red brick jeans. I saw a pair of jeans today the color of red bricks, with little black highlights, like something had faded into them. You'd look good in something like that."

"Thanks," she said.

"Only sensual people look good in red. Did you know that?"

Autumn shook her head. "No."

"Which means you're probably a very sensual person. There's a way to find out for sure, though."

She swallowed and gave him what she knew was probably a deer-in-headlights look.

"Don't worry," he said and held out his hand. "It doesn't involve doing anything your mother wouldn't approve of. All you have to do is let me see your hand." He nodded toward his. "Come on. It won't hurt a bit."

When she put her hand in his, he flipped it over and passed the pads of his four fingers quickly from the heel of her hand to the tips of her fingers.

"Now," he said. "There are people who feel very uncomfortable when people touch them and people who are just starving for touch, even if they already get a lot.

Each one of us is programmed to need a different amount of touch. And of course there are plenty of people in between. But you strike me as a woman of extremes. Now let's see which one you are."

With that he began tracing his fingertip lightly over her palm. The sensation sent a jolt of need right between her legs. Gradually, her hand began to open like a flower, until her fingers occupied the same plane as her palm. "Mm-hm," he said. "I was right about you. You are a sensualist. You opened up to me. If you were the other type, you would have curled your fingers, protecting your vulnerability." He held her gaze. "You enjoy being touched, don't you, Autumn?"

Her cheeks warmed. "This isn't where I'm supposed to be," she whispered.

"I know," he answered. "Believe me, I know. And that's exactly why you wouldn't choose to be anywhere else this moment."

She looked into her glass and remembered meeting Claudio for the first time and how afraid of him she had been. She'd been more afraid of not having anywhere to go. But now she had Adam and Maria.

And you want to leave them both.

Not yet, she told herself. It wasn't time yet. She shook her head. "I have to go," she said. "My friends are probably waking up and we have to figure out how to get where we're going."

Bill put his hand on her arm. "Maybe I can help. What kind of trouble are you having?" His tone was businesslike. For some reason that reassured her, even though he had the ability to hold her prisoner with a single touch.

"It's just money. We don't have much money. And we don't really know where we're going."

"Are you on the run from somebody?"

Autumn nodded. "My uh, ex. He's...I'm afraid he's going to come after us. So we have to get far away and...I don't know why I'm telling you this." She slid out of the booth and stood up.

"Listen," he said, leaning forward. "I don't normally do this, but you seem like a nice girl who's fallen on hard times. And I'm a guy who has certain…needs, if you get my drift. So I'll make you an offer. A hundred dollars to come back to my place."

She stared at him, dumbfounded. "You're offering me money to sleep with you?"

"Yes, and no. I want to do more than sleep with you. I'm kind of a kinky guy and most girls don't want to get as intense as I do."

"Why don't you hire a prostitute?"

"Because," he said, sliding out of the booth and standing. Autumn backed away a few steps. "It's pretty hard to find someone who'll do what I want who is as pretty as you."

"What makes you think I'd do whatever it is you want?"

"I don't. That's why I'm asking. You need something, and I need something, and we could come to an agreement and help each other out."

Autumn looked down. She couldn't believe he was suggesting she hire herself out for money like that. "I don't…I'm not like that."

"Then what are you like? You said you wanted an adventure, right? This doesn't mean anything. It's just two people helping each other out." He bent his knees to get a better look at her face. "Aren't you even curious as to what I want?"

She looked up at him. "What?"

"I want to spank you."

Chills like cold spikes pricked all over her body.

"Have you ever been spanked before—by a man?"

She nodded.

"Well, then you know what I'm talking about. It turns me on like nothing else. I want to pull your pants down, put you over my knee and spank that cute little ass of yours. Then I want to make love to you."

"You can't find anyone to do that?"

He bowed his head and smiled. "I won't lie. It doesn't stop there. I want to get pretty rough. I want to use my belt. I want to talk to you like you've been very bad and you're getting what you deserve. I don't want to lead you to my place and surprise you and have you freak out. So. What do you think?"

Autumn trembled. Claudio had punished her like that. But the thought of being at his mercy intensified her desire.

"I won't come back to your place for a hundred dollars," she said.

He shrugged. "That's understandable. You don't know me. I'm just some guy you met in a bar on the dark side of Bourbon Street. But consider this," he said, coming closer. The low, scratchy rumbling of his voice held her. He reached around and massaged her neck. "I'm willing to up it to two hundred. And I promise not to hurt you much. I know what I'm doing. And I know what I'm saying is making you hot for me."

His hand traveled down her back and grasped her rear, squeezing lightly. Her breath hitched. "I won't..."

He put his free hand on the back of her neck and pulled her forward into a kiss. A warm man-smell mixed with the scents of cigarettes and beer, old cologne and stale bars. His tongue nudged its way gently into her mouth until she returned the kiss hungrily. Then he ended it and pulled her close. "I want to show you how hot you are," he whispered.

"I won't do it for two hundred," she whispered back. "But I'll do it for five."

He squeezed the back of her neck. She pulled away.

"Hundred," she added. "Five hundred. No less."

He nodded. "Okay," he said. "But I get to do whatever I want."

Autumn nodded.

Bill reached back, picked up her glass and handed it to her. "Drink up," he said. "You don't want to waste good stuff."

She nodded, and took small, quick swallows. It was very good. And it settled her fears. So what if his desires mirrored Claudio's? She would be able to leave when it was over, and she and the others would have a little extra money in their stash. Besides, she told herself, Bill was pretty attractive, and that deep scratchy voice was sexy.

And it wasn't as though she'd never felt a belt before.

Chapter Five

BILL LIVED in a French Quarter apartment he said he'd had for a long time. One corner of his living room had a small bar built into it, with a shelf on the wall behind it full of bottles with liquids at varying levels. Guitars filled another corner.

"Guess which one is my favorite," he said on the way to the bar, when he saw her looking at them.

"That one," she said, pointing to a battered-looking black Stratocaster, trying to distract herself from wondering just what this guy wanted from her. She wondered what would happen if she apologized and made for the door. Would he come after her?

"Yep," he said, taking a couple of shot glasses from underneath the bar and setting them on the surface.

She looked at him quickly, wondering how he'd known the questions in her mind. Then she remembered she'd given him an answer to his guitar question.

"How did you know?" he asked. "The other ones look so much more cared for."

"My ex is a musician," she said, looking at the guitars, trying not to let her voice tremble. "And his favorite instrument was an old violin. It got pretty scratched from being used all the time. Somebody took it, though."

Bill had started scrutinizing his bottles, but her comment made him turn around quickly. "*Took* it?"

The urgency in his voice made Autumn turn to him, spinning on one heel with the toes of that foot in the air, the other foot remaining planted, pretending to be bolder than she felt. She bit her lip and thrust her head forward, looking at him. The concern on his face was almost humorous. It put her at ease—but only a little. She shrugged and turned back to the instruments, thinking she was probably overreacting. She reached out and touched the Stratocaster with her fingertip, leaving a slight smudge. "He made another vam…another guy mad and…he took it. My ex is like that. That's why I left."

"Because he lost his violin?" Bill said, turning back to the bottles and choosing one that contained a clear liquid.

"No," Autumn said, wandering away from the guitar to look at the framed posters on Bill's walls of the Stones and Dire Straits, kicking herself for moving away from the door and talking out of nervousness. "Because he's just…I don't know. He likes to push people. Plus, he's a pretty scary guy."

Kinda like you, she thought. She wanted the hint of real danger, and that had made it necessary for her to get involved with Claudio, and to come here today. She wanted to throw herself into situations she would need to escape from later.

Autumn watched Bill closely as he poured the clear liquid into each of the shot glasses and brought them around, handing one to her. "Cheers," he said, and shot his, watching her with a curious little smile on his face.

He's going to do anything he wants, she told herself. *Whether I want him to or not.*

Autumn lifted her glass, sized him up while looking for reassurance about shooting the drink, and lost her nerve just as the liquid touched her lips.

"Just send it to the back of your throat if you don't like it. It's tequila."

"Oh," she said, and closed her eyes. It went down, but she sputtered and coughed against the back of her wrist, looking at him sheepishly.

He held out his hand.

She stared at it for a moment, unsure of what he wanted, then she nodded and handed him her glass.

"You're not much of a drinker, are you?" he said, and took both back to the bar, setting them down so carefully the glass barely knocked the wood.

She shook her head. "No, not...not really."

"But you do other things," he said. He lowered his voice and made his way over to her, sending the butterflies in her stomach into a frenzy. "Bad things."

Autumn swallowed and looked at the door.

When he put his arms around her, Autumn felt his erection through his pants. She pulled away and searched for an escape route.

"I'm not letting you go," he said. "You're here now. You want this." He held her tighter and squeezed her bottom with both hands, hard.

Yes! I want this. This is what I want...

"You think it's wise to go to a strange guy's apartment? Huh? Looks like somebody's going to have to teach you a little lesson about proper behavior for a young lady."

Within seconds, he had her skirt down. It puddled at her feet. He kissed her forehead and lowered his lips to her ear. "Know what I'm going to do with you?" he asked "I'm going to put you over my knee and spank your ass. That's what I'm going to do. Come home with a strange man and that's what you get. Then I'm going to take off my belt and give you some more."

She wondered just what she had gotten herself into, but her body collapsed against his and she began to sway with him, falling into the sound of his breathing and the feel of his warmth through the suit. She opened her lips. She was beyond escape, and she knew it. He squeezed her bare flesh, lightly at first, then harder. It made her whimper.

"Like that?" he said, and squeezed until shards of pain radiated in every direction. Then he tickled his fingers along the cheek until she gasped. He moved closer and closer to her openings, his fingertips circling like sharks. "What a bad girl," he rasped. "Little slut wants it. Little sluts have to be punished," he said.

She whimpered again at his words, just as his fingers moved aside the thin strip of her panties and slid into her pussy. He worked them in and out and let her press against his erection.

"Please," she found herself saying. "Please fuck me." Hearing the words come out of her mouth surprised her, but she was desperate to climax, desperate to have this man inside her.

"Mm-mm," he said. "Not until after you get what you deserve." He took her by the arms and pushed her out of the embrace, then sat on the couch and took her over his lap so quickly, she couldn't help but struggle with the shock of it all. He held her in place and calmed her by rubbing his hand in circles on her bare bottom. Her skin hummed. Then his hand was gone and the next thing she knew, he'd brought it down hard enough to make her yelp.

"Shh…" he said. "Don't get too loud. We don't want the neighbors to get worried. You're going to want to save that for when it really hurts." He brought his hand down again on the same spot with a report like pistol fire, and paused for a moment. She tried to catch her breath. *Oh God,* she thought, wanting it to stop. Wanting it to be over so she could hide in some corner somewhere and think about what had happened, and maybe touch herself a little. But now it hurt. Now the pops hit her ears and made her want to struggle away from him, especially when he began giving her quick, hard smacks, warming up one spot before moving to another. She squirmed and reached back to protect her bottom. He captured her wrist and held it behind her back, then continued with the spanking.

"Please..." she said, out of breath. "It hurts."

Bill paused and rubbed her bottom with his hand, stroking the tender flesh with his fingertips. "It's supposed to hurt, Autumn. I thought you had been spanked before. Or did you lie to me?"

He smacked her hard to accentuate that last sentence. She couldn't help yelping. "Someone didn't do his job with you. I'd love to have you to myself for a few weeks. I'd teach you a few things, like how to take a real spanking." He gave her another hard pop and another, until tears came to her eyes. Then he began teasing her slit with his fingertip. "Let me see what a bad girl you are," he said. "Let me see how wet you can get for me."

He slipped in his finger. She couldn't help but moan and move her hips around on his thigh. "Do you want me to fuck you, Autumn?"

She could reply only by nodding her head. She shook all over. Bill slid his finger out again, teased her opening some more, and slid it in and out while she lay across his knee and made deep noises of longing, animal noises that were in her body long before she had ever learned words. Her bottom stung wherever he brushed it with his hand or his sleeve, but it only added to the pleasure she felt as he played with her. Longing mixed with dread made her whimper.

"I don't hear you," he said, still working her slit.

"Yes..." she was barely able to say.

"Beg me."

"Please fuck me. Please..."

"That's more like it," he said. "Get up."

The abrupt command stunned her, but she got off his lap and stood with shaky legs, looking for her skirt.

"No," he said. "You can't have it yet. Stand there just like that, in your shirt. I want you to watch me take off my belt." As he spoke, his hands went to the buckle. The hair all over Autumn's body stood on end. If the spanking had hurt, what was this going to feel like? She wondered if she shouldn't have just gone back to the hotel. Adam and Maria would probably be waking up soon.

Autumn jumped at the swish Bill's belt made when he took it off. She began to tremble harder as he looped it in his hand. "Turn around. Get on your knees. Bend over the couch."

She shook her head. "I…"

"You agreed to do this," he said. "Now do it."

The tone of his voice made her body hot and cold at the same time. She nodded and did as he said, burying her face in one of the pillows, trying to swallow. Her throat froze when the belt made contact with her bottom. She couldn't breathe. It was desperation that made her take a deep breath just as the belt made contact a second time. She squeezed her eyes shut tight and balled her hands into fists as the belt came down again and again. She pictured what Bill must look like whipping her. It was a frightening image, and made her want to hide. It also made her very, very wet.

When it was over, he tossed the belt on the couch and grabbed her by the upper arms, maneuvering her backward into a standing position, pulling her against him, whispering into her ear. "That's one of the things that bad girls get," he said, before quickly tugging her shirt over her head. Then he lay her on the floor and ran a lascivious gaze over her bare body, reaching into his jacket pocket and tossing a couple of condoms onto the floor beside her. He undressed himself quickly and tossed the clothes aside.

He had an attractive body, slim and slightly muscular, with a little dusting of light brown hair on his chest and stomach. He kept his eyes on her as he ripped open the condom and rolled it onto his cock, enticing Autumn with the smell of latex.

He rubbed the lubricated head against her opening, spreading her own juices all over her pussy. She opened her legs wide for him as he settled on top of her and entered her easily. "Is this what you wanted?" he asked. "You wanted me to fuck you?"

She nodded vigorously, already panting for him.

He kept himself raised on his hands as he slid in and out of her slowly. It drove her crazy. She couldn't help but thrash around on his cock, wanting it harder, letting the desperation show in her eyes. "Please," she whispered again and again.

"Please what?" he asked, a little smile playing on his lips.

"Please…" was all she could say.

Eventually, he gave her what she wanted and began pumping into her, making her backside rub against the rough surface of the rug, which hurt her pinked flesh pleasantly. She wanted to throw back her head and close her eyes to concentrate on the intense sensation of this strange man's dick violating her—that was the fantasy, that he had made her come here, that she didn't have a choice—but she also wanted to look at his face as he fucked her. She made herself watch him alternately tense his jaw and press his lips together, then slacken those lips and roll back his eyes.

His bare chest smelled of last night's sweat. She wanted it pressed against her, but she didn't dare move.

Finally, he stopped pumping into her and lowered himself onto his elbows to whisper in her ear. "Is this what you like? Strange men fucking you?"

Autumn nodded. He slid his arms under her shoulders and pulled her back onto his cock as he ground into her, pressing against clit and labia, bringing her close to climax. He was everywhere—on her, in her, around her.

Again, she surprised herself by speaking. "Tell me…"

"Tell you what?" he asked before pressing his lips together. It was an expression she found very attractive on him.

"Tell me…I can't get away…"

He smiled. "You're a little captive girl, huh? Well, you made the mistake of going with a strange man into his apartment and now he's fucking you and you can't get away. I'm not letting you go until I'm finished with you."

Autumn turned her head to the side so she couldn't see him anymore. The intensity was too much, but she didn't want it to stop. The sound of his voice made her moan.

"I can do anything to you that I want to," he said between clenched teeth. "I can tie you down and fuck you for days, stick my dick into your pussy until you scream."

The electric warmth between her legs exploded in a painful orgasm that made her cry out with a sound halfway between a moan and a scream. Then she lay there panting and looking at him, thinking that this was the man who had done that to her.

He smiled and kissed her. "Beautiful," he said and pulled out, shocking her with emptiness. "Get on all fours."

Her body shook with spent emotion as she got up and turned around for him, felt him position his cock at her opening and ease himself in. Once inside, he grabbed her hips and began pumping her hard. "Oh…oh, yeah," he rumbled. His voice seemed even more gravelly as his pleasure heightened. Her body felt helpless as he impaled her again and again, taking his pleasure, sticking it deep. Finally, he growled and slowed his pace, pulling her hard against him once, then again, stabbing his cock into her, then shoving it all the way in and holding it there.

Autumn lowered the front half of her body onto her elbows and took deep breaths, wondering if this made her a slut. She asked herself if she cared enough not to do it, and the answer was no. She felt something inside her wake up.

Bill pulled out of her. She kept her position, more out of habit than anything else. Claudio had always demanded she not move until he gave her permission. It took a few seconds for Autumn to remember this wasn't Claudio, and he probably wasn't going to punish her if she moved. So she did, sitting on her hip with her legs curled behind her, watching him unsheathe his penis from the condom. He tied the top and put it aside to move toward her on all fours and kiss her on the lips.

"Did you like it?" he asked.

Autumn gave him a shy smile and nodded, lowering her head submissively. Strands of red hair fell toward her face. She put it behind her ear. "I liked it," she said.

"I liked it too," he said. "If you ever want a repeat performance, just ask anyone in any Bourbon Street bar where to find me. I'm not hard to find."

She nodded. On a whim, she moved toward Bill and kissed him, slipping her tongue into his mouth. She could tell it surprised him, but he kissed her back enthusiastically before she pulled away and smiled. "I have to go now," she said.

"I guess you do," he said, and got up. "Don't go yet." She watched him curiously as he opened the door and walked naked into the next room, running her eyes down his back and rear, musing that that body had just been all over her and that she probably smelled like him now. She was mostly dressed when he came back.

"This is actually all the cash I have in the house," he said, handing her a stack of twenties. "It's five hundred."

She looked at it, then shook her head. "I…I can't…"

"Don't think of it like that," he said. "Think of it as us helping each other out. If I see you again, by the way, I'm not paying for it. In fact, *you'll* owe *me* dinner."

She looked at him. His expression was earnest.

"For your friends," he said. "To help get you far away from that guy."

"Thanks," she said. "But really. I can't. I know we talked about it at the bar, but…I just…it's not me."

"Yes," he said. "You can."

She stood there for a moment, holding the stacks of cash. It was an awful lot of money for someone in her position. She and the others needed all they could get at this point. Promising herself that this would be the only time, she nodded, accepted his hug, grabbed her little pack and ambled out the door.

Downstairs, Autumn stood blinking in the afternoon light. He had let her go. The only reason she was standing outside at that moment was that he had decided to let her go. He could just as easily have decided to make her stay, and that thought made her too weak to stand on her own. She leaned against the building and closed her eyes.

At some point, unsure how long she had been there, Autumn started walking. It was two in the afternoon, and she figured the biscuits and cheese had probably melted into an unidentifiable goo by now. She had been too excited today to feel hungry and her stomach was only now starting to twinge.

She wondered if part of that twinge wasn't because she felt really odd about having just rented out her body.

Then she forgot about it again in favor of wondering if Tina would brag to her friends about meeting a vampire, and if they would believe her. There were so many things to feel anxious about today. Either way, Autumn reasoned, it was probably best for them to leave and find a safe place. There had to be some refuges for vampires who were out on their own, she thought. And she could probably Google them. The Internet café Tina had pointed out the night before wasn't far away.

A well-dressed man walked behind her with the unhurried assurance of a master predator.

The Internet café was an oddly shabby place full of old computers, but Autumn planned to be there only for a moment. She paid a young guy with a long, wispy forelock and lip piercings for an hour and sat down, then looked around to make sure no one was standing nearby. In a room of about fifteen computers facing two bright yellow paint-peeled walls, there were only about six people, including herself and a chubby girl who had pulled up a chair near a pot-bellied, middle-aged man Autumn assumed was her father.

Each new thing felt more interesting, exciting and worrisome than the last.

Finally, she typed in, "Where is a safe place for vampires in New Orleans?" in the Google search bar and waited. The first thing she saw was New Orleans Spirit Tours, then New Orleans Vampire and guides to New Orleans.

She didn't find what she was looking for until the second page.

The site was called Biali's: Vampire Restaurant and Resort. The blurb read, "Network with your own kind and enjoy a meal away from the hassles of living with the Others."

Autumn clicked on it, and was surprised to find a black page with purple writing that simply asked: "When can a vampire make another vampire?" Below that was a bright white reply box. Autumn stared at it for a moment, then looked around, fearful that someone might be looking over her shoulder, but the one person she could see clearly from her spot, a pretty woman who looked to be in her early thirties, wearing jeans and her hair pinned atop her head, seemed hypnotized by her own computer screen. Autumn typed, "When he or she is in phase."

She hit enter and waited. "One moment please..." came the reply, before a plain white page with black writing appeared. "For the welfare of all vampires and those who associate with them, the management asks that you share this page with no one who is not in the community. We are a haven for those in need of assistance, and an oasis for those in need of companionship. If you have never visited our establishment before, please give us a call at the number below and tell us your situation."

Autumn took down the number and went to one of the three wall phones near the snack machine. She supposed the phones were for guests who didn't want to put certain types of calls on their cells. She backed into the corner made by the wall and the large black machine, enjoying the sensation of cool metal against her arm, and firm sheetrock against her back, hoping for at least a little privacy.

A woman's polished voice answered, surprising her.

"Um...hello?" Autumn said.

"Yes?" the voice answered. "Whom are you trying to reach?" Her accent was Northern, but Autumn couldn't place it.

"I'm...I'm calling about Biali's. I...have a situation to explain." It felt like a dumb thing to say, but she couldn't think of anything better. She stared at the backs of other patrons to distract herself. The girl with the older man shifted in her seat and moved her book pack around at her feet. She was in a light-blue sweater.

What an unprovocative color, Autumn thought. It was the sort of color a girl wore if she had never gone home with a strange man and taken money for sex, she supposed.

"Okay," the voice said. "What is your role?"

"My role?" Autumn asked, looking away from the girl and blinking rapidly. Her heart sped. What if the woman didn't believe her?

"What *are* you? Are you one of us?" The woman made her voice slightly more urgent.

"Not...not exactly," Autumn said. For a moment, she wondered if Biali's was just some club for people who liked to pretend to be vampires, maybe a high-class fetish establishment. She blushed. "I'm a...well, I *was* a...a feeder."

There was a pause, then the woman said, "I see. Why are you calling us? What do you need?"

Motion at the front door caught her eye. A man in a gray suit with bleached blond hair sauntered in, paused and removed his sunglasses, taking stock of the room. Autumn could have sworn she saw him sniff the air. He raised his nose first in one direction, then in another, a gesture she had seen vampires make many times. Then she decided she was freaking out so much her eyes were playing tricks on her, especially when the man made his way over to the snack machine and dropped in a few quarters.

"Are you there?" the woman on the phone asked. Autumn hadn't realized she'd zoned out.

"Oh," she said, holding the phone with both hands, cradling it against her chin. "I'm...I'm sorry."

By now, only the man's shoulder and one arm were visible around the snack machine, but she heard him punch a button.

Autumn lowered her voice, hoping the phone connection was good enough for the woman to hear. Even vampire ears couldn't make up for a faulty connection. "We need a safe place to go. My friend is...one of you...and he...*bit* someone last night. She liked it, but I'm worried she may tell someone. You never know how people will talk."

Autumn leaned forward to try to see if the guy's body language revealed he had heard anything, but she still couldn't see much. The thump and rattle of his selection hitting the tray made her jump. He leaned forward and squeaked open the top.

"No, you don't," the woman said. She still spoke in a clipped manner but Autumn thought her voice had softened just a little. "Do you have a pen?"

"Yes," Autumn said, and shrugged out of her little pack. The plastic bag inside rattled and smelled like grease. She found a pen and a scrap of paper and took down the address and directions, plus an additional phone number.

The man backed away from the machine, leaned to the side and looked at her. His eyes were a bright turquoise blue. He looked her over, twitched his lips into a smile, and left. He sauntered across the room with a honey bun in one hand and his sunglasses in the other. He paused at Autumn's computer. She felt as though she were on fire.

"The day you are planning to come, call this number for the password. It changes each day, for obvious reasons."

"Okay," Autumn said suddenly, shaking herself out of her stupor. "Thank you."

After hanging up, she inched from around the snack machine, watching the man. No one else in the room seemed to notice him. Even the guy at the counter gave him only a cursory glance before going back to his book.

Finally, the man simply left without looking at her again. Shaken, Autumn hurried over to the computer, kicking herself for not closing the window before making the call. She scanned the screen to see if maybe the site's URL was on the page anywhere. It wasn't on the page, but it was in the window at the top of the page. She logged out hurriedly and looked at the door, her heart thumping madly. She didn't see him, but that didn't mean he wasn't right around the corner.

Whoever he was.

Chapter Six

ADAM STOOD with both hands planted on his head, staring at Autumn, who sat on the bed with the stack of twenties beside her. The biscuits and cheese sat, still wrapped, on top of the plastic sack at the writing desk, where Maria sat and watched with a sad, worried look on her face.

Autumn forced herself to focus on the leaf on Adam's ancient red Adidas T-shirt so she wouldn't think about how foolish she felt. Suddenly, he turned around, raised both arms in frustration and turned back to stare at Autumn some more.

"Please don't tell me I just heard you correctly," Adam said. "Because if you actually slept with some jackass out there for money, I will lose my mind. Please tell me that ain't what you just said."

Autumn looked down at the rumpled bedspread, feeling humiliated. She had almost told them about the strange man in the Internet café, but for some reason the words wouldn't come out. And now Adam was so upset about Bill, she didn't think she could add to it. "I didn't sleep with him for money. I slept with him because I wanted to. We just helped each other out, that's all." Her voice was quiet.

He raised his finger. Then he lowered it again. "You prostituted yourself," he said.

"I don't see what the difference is," she said. Tears pricked her eyes. "I slept with Claudio…and you…and Seth…and Chloe…all those years to have somewhere to stay. Why can't I do it with some guy one time to make our trip easier?"

"Because you don't *do* things like that, Autumn. It's not something you do."

She turned her eyes up to him. "Why?"

"Because I said so, that's why."

She looked down at the money. Her eyes filled with tears. "Are you going to punish me?" she asked. In spite of the games she had played with Bill, she was just a little worried about the prospect of real punishment, but the question came out as a challenge.

"No," Adam said, sounding perturbed. "I don't do that, and you know it. I just wish you hadn't done *this,* is all." He gestured at the money as though it were diseased. Autumn wondered if he thought of her that way now, and was much more alarmed by the prospect than she thought she would be.

"Well, it's done now," Maria said, standing up and making her way to Autumn. "We might as well make the best of it. Use the money to go somewhere."

Autumn looked up at Maria gratefully and put her hand on Maria's as the other woman sat next to her and put her arm around Autumn's shoulders. She wasn't prepared for the pain she saw in Maria's eyes, in spite of the forgiving smile. It was unlike Maria to be so warm. It made her feel guilty to think she was the only person that inspired Maria's gentler side, and now she was thinking of ripping that away from her. The notion startled her.

I am, aren't I? she thought. *That really is what I'm considering.*

Something knotted in her chest until she could hardly breathe. "Yeah," Autumn said, and pulled away to stand up, wiping at her eyes. "That's what we should do. Just forget this happened and use the money. I won't do it again."

"Fair enough," Adam said.

"I have this too," Autumn said, reaching into her bag for the Biali House information and offering the scrap of paper to Adam. "I Googled 'safe places for vampires' and they made me jump through a bunch of hoops. The site won't even let you in unless you can tell them a vampire has to be in phase to make another vampire...or, I assume it won't. It asked the question and I answered and it let me in."

Adam took the paper and looked at it. "That's not too far away. I wonder if it's for real."

"You have to call the other number the day you're coming because they change the password every day."

"It could be a trap," Maria said. "I'm sure there are people out there who know about vampires and don't like them."

Autumn thought again about the man in the Internet café. She knew she should tell them, but simply couldn't bring herself to. She had never actually handled things before and didn't want anything to ruin the fact that she had actually found a solution to one of their problems, a place for them to go. At least, that's what she told herself. She refused to think about the fact that there was something enticingly dangerous about the man, something familiar.

Adam nodded. "True. But would they do this, or would they do something else? In my experience, when it comes to racism, most people like to get other people worked up so they can spend their time talking shit. They'd start a movement. It takes an extremely fucked-up individual to go to that much trouble just to hurt people. I think it's more likely to be what it says it is."

"Why didn't Claudio ever mention anything like that?" Maria asked.

"Claudio played everything close," Adam said, grabbing his bag from the floor and shoving in yesterday's T-shirt. "We were all on a need-to-know basis. He probably knows a lot more than he ever told any of us."

"And now we have to figure it out by ourselves?" Maria asked. "He made sure we couldn't survive without him. What kind of man is that?"

"Hel-lo-o..." Autumn sing-songed irritably, her humiliation gone. "I've found a place to go. We're going to do all right on our own."

"Unless, like I said, it's a trap." Maria hunched down and crossed her arms. "The world isn't just a pretty little garden for you to play in, you know, Autumn. There are bad people out there. Even if that place *is* for vampires, what makes you think *we'll* be welcome there?"

Autumn glared back at her. "We have to go to find out. You're the one who wanted to take your chances out in the world. That's what I'm doing. I want to experience things. And yes, even strange men in New Orleans bars."

Maria started to open her mouth, but Autumn shook her head, leaning slightly forward as she talked.

"I'm not some stupid, innocent kid. Sure, there's plenty I don't know, and I'll probably make mistakes, but I want to *do* things. My things," she said, patting her chest. "Not just follow you around like a puppy. And if something bad happens to me because of that, then so be it. At least I was free for a while. If we don't enjoy what we're doing out here, and...and...take the bull by the horns, then we should have stayed with Claudio, where it's nice and safe." She turned to Adam. "Are we going to Biali House or not?"

Adam sighed and nodded. "I guess so. Ain't like we have anyplace else."

* * * *

Biali House turned out to be a posh resort with a long, curving concrete drive uphill that led to a checkpoint at a large iron gate flanked by white stone pillars mounted by dancing cherubs. Autumn, Adam and Maria walked up the incline in a cluster of people wearing jeans, travel pants and T-shirts. Behind them, a car honked. Adam moved out of the way and scowled over his shoulder at the well-dressed man with sandy hair in a slicked-back World War II Era do, who gave him a smug smile and then flashed his fangs. A woman in a mini dress sat beside him with her hand on his crotch.

Adam scowled harder. "Probably ain't changed that ugly-assed hairstyle in forty years either," he muttered. "And you know what? Cats that old probably have some pretty outdated attitudes about a few things."

"Sixty years," Maria said.

"What?"

"That style hasn't been popular for sixty years."

"Whatever," Adam said. "It's ugly, and the cats who wore it back then were...oh, never mind. Fuck it. I don't care."

Both Autumn and Maria looked at him strangely. "I didn't realize this was going to be such a huge trip to the past for you," Maria said, accidentally stepping off the side of the concrete and nearly losing her balance.

Autumn instinctively reached out for her, but Maria pulled away. "I'm fine," she muttered. Autumn, who had gotten over her anger, nodded and blinked back tears, swallowing a lump in her throat, annoyed that it had hurt her feelings.

"A past I'd like to forget," Adam said. "Things weren't so great back then. Why do you think I said yes when Claudio waltzed in and asked me if I'd like to be a vampire?"

"He *asked* you?" Autumn said, glad for something other than Maria to think about.

"Sure, he asked me. Pointed out I didn't stand a chance in hell of getting anywhere in life unless I could put a few decades under my belt and still be young. So I said yes."

"Was it worth it?" Maria asked.

"Abso-fucking-lutely," Adam said.

"Language, language," Maria said absently, looking off in another direction.

To avoid looking at her, Autumn supposed. She wished things could feel normal again for a while.

A uniformed man at the gate mechanically asked for the password, then passed hungry eyes over Maria and Autumn hungrily. He had a slight build, with high cheekbones and short black hair. His skin was pale. Maria frowned at him, while Autumn met his gaze curiously. He appeared to be in his mid-twenties, but his eyes seemed much older. All at once he looked down and smiled sheepishly. "Forgive me. The hunger comes upon me suddenly and I don't have a break for two more hours. No offense meant."

"None taken," Maria said.

Autumn simply stared, barely aware he was speaking, wondering how old he really was and what it would be like to tempt him.

"Yeah, well just keep it under control, brother," Adam said.

The man nodded at him. "Of course. You'll want to take the right pathway and go around to the back entrance."

"The *what?*" Adam said.

"I'm sorry," the man answered. "There is a dress code to use the front entrance, and for access to many of the areas in the house. Plus, in order to stay here for free, each feeder must provide at least one meal to guests or staff per week. It's all explained in this brochure."

"Provide a meal?" Maria said. "You've got to be kidding. How are we going to get away from this life if..."

"Shh..." Adam said, taking the brochure from the guard. "This may not be the best place to discuss this. Let's go in, get our room and then figure out what to do, okay? Maybe we can talk to the management."

Maria nodded and looked down. Autumn felt bad for her, and felt guilty that she was excited to be here when the others were so obviously distressed. She took a brochure with a big smile at the vampire, who simply returned the smile, nodded and turned to the next people in line. Then she bounded the two steps to Adam and hugged his arm. "I think it's going to be fun," she said.

"Right," Adam replied. "Fun."

Maria stared at the ground all the way up the walkway.

They were received in a large, elegant room with about thirty other people in travel and hiking clothes. Some of them hadn't shaved for days and wore ball caps over oily hair. Autumn tried to figure out which were the vampires and which were the feeders, just from the way they stood. A guy in a faded red Mohawk gave her a menacing stare, nodded his head in a challenge and mouthed, "What are you looking at?" At first she thought he had to be a vampire, but then she noticed the bar code tattoo on the side of his neck. Vampires couldn't have tattoos. As a blonde woman in a faded wife-beater shirt smacked him on the arm with the back of her hand. He backed off and stood with his hands clasped in front and head down, but still looked at Autumn out of the corner of his eye like a dog that would have liked nothing more than to take a chunk out of her throat.

"These are not attractive people," Maria whispered to her.

Pleasantly startled, Autumn looked to find Maria offering her a hesitant smile. "Tell me about it," she whispered back. "The feeders look meaner than the vampires."

"Will you two keep it down?" Adam whispered. "Let's just see what's going on. We seem to be waiting for something."

"Or someone," Autumn said excitedly. She looked around. The ceilings were a good twenty feet high, with heavy chandeliers and antique, hand-carved furnishings polished to a high gloss and kept around the perimeter of the room, behind blue velvet rope. The walls were lined with shelves and filled with antique implements from daily life like dishes and spectacles. According to the brochure, it was known as the "Secondary Receiving Room."

Except for explanations of the process the wealthy Italian entrepreneur Federico Biali went through to contract and build the house in 1890, and its evolution into a private club for the very rich, there wasn't a lot of information in the brochure. There was no mention of vampires or networking. Autumn guessed they wanted to minimize the amount of information that actually left the premises, and having brochures all over the place touting a meeting place for vampires wasn't the best way to be discreet.

In spite of the lack of concrete information about the club or the management, however, Autumn found the brochure fascinating, and had to be elbowed out of her stupor by Adam when a man came through a door that led into the room via a round set of stairs, and remained on the pinnacle.

He had pale skin and high cheekbones. He wore a top hat and a black leather jacket over a purple T-shirt, with more accessories than Autumn had ever seen on a guy in her life. He stood there a moment before speaking, hands clasped in front, looking at each person in the crowd, taking his time, nodding a little. Gradually, the talking stopped. Everyone turned to him.

"Good afternoon," he said, in a pleasant, yet no-nonsense, voice. "My name is Mick, and I am one of the managers of Biali House. If you have a problem during your stay here, or if you need something—anything at all—you just need to find me or one of my assistants..." He gestured around the room to about a dozen people, mostly men, posted around the perimeter of the room, dressed similarly to Mick. "...and we will take care of things for you."

Autumn thought they looked like a very large rock band that belonged in the eighties. Her stomach squirmed pleasantly.

"In case any of you are wondering," Mick said, "I am a vampire. My assistants are vampires, and I work directly with our host, Freddie Biali, whom many of you probably know is actually the officially 'late' Federico Biali. The official story that we give to the outside world, of course, is that Freddie is Federico's great-great nephew. Every few decades or so, he has to go into hiding, only to re-emerge in a different persona. We like to tease him about that. Our nickname for him is the Great Locust, but..." And here he lowered his voice to a whisper and put a finger near his lips. "Don't tell him." He gave the audience a conspiratorial nod. Many of them laughed. Autumn noticed he was wearing eyeliner. When he turned his head to the side, she could see that his sandy hair was pulled back into a ponytail. It hung just below his shoulders.

"Here's the deal," he said, raising his hands to gesture with his fingers splayed, showing off black-polished nails. Before he could continue, however, someone interrupted.

"How old are you?" called a woman from the crowd.

He smiled. "Every single day at least one person asks me that question. And it just had to be you, didn't it? Where are you from?"

"San Antonio," the woman said.

"Have you been here before?" he asked.

"No."

"Of course you haven't, or you'd know all my secrets by now." He pointed at an attractive Indian guy with curly hair wearing a pink shirt. "I know you've been here before. I don't recognize anyone else out there. To answer your question, I'm five hundred and seventy-two years old, a little older than our host. Astounding, isn't it? And yet I've managed to continue to fit in, as time passes. It's why I managed to live this long. That, and vampires are *really* hard to kill. As for Freddie, he's a good friend of mine and we've known each other practically forever. He addresses the guests twice a week at the common dinners in the Great Hall, to which everyone is invited, and of course enjoys speaking to our guests, so if you would like to meet him, the next one is…" He reached into the inside pocket of his jacket and pulled out a PDA. He turned it on and grinned at the crowd. "Technology and vampires, right? The next one is…tomorrow?" He poked around with the stylus.

"It's tonight," called out one of the assistants—a young-looking Asian man in a white suit.

"Ah! Tonight," Mick said, looking at the screen. "Ah, yes. Tonight. You think you *feeders* have a hard time keeping up with the days of the week. If you ever get to be my age, whew! Let me tell you." He put the PDA away and brought his hands together enthusiastically. "Okay, so tonight, Freddie will be addressing everyone. We'll get some room assignments going, where you'll find laminated booklets with all the information you'll need about prices and costs and which activities you're eligible for and areas of the house you're allowed in. I'm assuming most of you are free boarders?"

The Indian guy raised his hand. "Actually, I'm a Gold customer. I don't know why they wanted me to come in this way."

"It's the blue jeans, man. They send everybody in jeans to me. You do know, though, there is a pimped-out dress code to most of the Gold functions, right?"

"I sent my clothes here beforehand."

"Oh, okay," Mick said, wagging his finger at him to come up. "We'll just get you to the right place. Everybody else, just hold tight and my assistants and myself will get your information...Oh, before I forget, I would also like to mention that in addition to helping guests feel welcome here at Biali House, I give seminars on fitting in and keeping up with the culture and social mores and not talking like a dusty old artifact and all that good stuff, so everybody make sure you get my card before you leave."

* * * *

A half-hour later, the three were in a suite three times the size of their hotel room, with a queen-sized bed under a royal blue canopy and matching chairs. "If this is what they give to freeloaders like us, I wonder what they give to the real guests," Adam grumped as he dumped his things on the mattress.

Autumn plopped down beside him. "We *are* real guests. This place is here to help people get on their feet as much as it is to give them a place to show off."

Adam held up his saxophone. "Eighty-plus years old and all I got to show for it is a beat-up old horn."

"You have us," Autumn offered.

"Yeah, well. Not for long," he said, and put down the instrument. "I'm going to shower and change. I think my spare jeans can hold up through one more wear. Then one of you has to find a washer and dryer."

"One of us?" Maria said, putting her hand on her hip. "Why can't you do it?"

"I'm old school," he said. "Two of you ain't feeding me, least you can do is my laundry." At the bathroom door, he turned around. "Ain't feeding me? Hell you ain't, if you're feeding these people in here we don't even know."

Autumn widened her eyes at him, surprised he would use such a bossy tone. For a moment, there was the hint of a jolt in her tummy, the beginning of a heat that would make its way down into her nether regions. But when Adam pawed at the air dismissively instead of following through on his demand, the feeling dissipated. Adam shook his head and mumbled his way into the bathroom.

"Wow," Maria said. "This thing is really affecting him."

Autumn watched the door close behind him, confused about her reaction. "It's affecting us all," she finally said.

Maria nodded and sat on the bed. "Yeah. I haven't said much about it, but…that thing with the money…sleeping with the guy…"

"I'm sorry," Autumn said, jumping at the opening. "You are the last person I would ever want to hurt, you and Adam."

Maria pressed her lips together. Her nose and eyes reddened. "That's what people always say before they drop a bombshell." She tried to smile, but wound up looking away and wiping at her eyes. "Shit."

Autumn went down on her knees in front of Maria, searching out her face. "I didn't know what I wanted back at Claudio's. How could I? That kind of life is all I've ever known. But now, I can do anything. I just…I want to experience things, Maria. And…" She sighed. "I think I'm going to have to go off on my own to do it."

"You like guys better?"

Autumn looked down. "I love you. I do. I just don't think I can keep being a couple with you. I want more freedom than that. I didn't want to hurt you."

Maria put her hand over her mouth and closed her eyes tight, but tears escaped anyway. Autumn tried to take her hand, but Maria stood up and waved her away. "I'm all right. I'm all right." She grabbed a tissue from the box on the nightstand. "I'll tell you what. I'm going to go for a walk for a while, okay? Tell Adam I'll be back in an hour, or two. You just...you just never know, do you?"

Autumn felt helpless as she watched Maria wipe her eyes in the mirror, straighten her top and fluff her hair. "Maria."

Maria turned and shook her head. "No. I don't want to hear right now. We'll talk later. I'll help you make yourself feel better then. But right now, I need my pain. Okay?"

She tossed her tissue in the trash and went out the door, leaving Autumn hugging her knees at the foot of the bed, listening to the roar of the shower, unsure what to do.

Next thing she knew, Adam was standing next to her with a towel wrapped around his hips, asking about Maria. Autumn shook her head. "Gone."

"Gone? What are you talking about?"

"She went for a walk. I, uh..." That was all she could get out before the tears came. "I..."

"Oh, baby girl," he said and sat next to her. He put his arm around her shoulders, squeezing her to him. "What's the matter?"

"I broke up with her."

"Come here," he said, even though she was already pressing against his side. "You two are too young to be taking all this so seriously."

"We're twenty-five and thirty."

"Well you know what I mean. She's hurt right now but she'll be okay. And you will too. You want to tell me why you broke up with her?"

Autumn shook her head. "I just don't want to be a couple with her anymore. It's too weird. It doesn't feel right. I love her, but I just need to be on my own for once in my life."

"I know the feeling, baby girl. I know the feeling. Listen, why don't you go and get cleaned up for dinner? I'm sure she'll be back by then. I'll talk to her tonight if you want to spend some time exploring, like I know you do. Okay?"

Autumn nodded. Once again, she'd managed to forget about everything other than her concerns about Maria and Adam, even the man from the Internet café.

He hadn't, however, forgotten about her.

Chapter Seven

THE BANQUET Hall seated five hundred guests in ten rows of tables, each accommodating fifty. At one end of the room, there was another table on a podium, with five empty chairs. Each table held a banquet of every kind of meat, bread, side dish and dessert imaginable.

Mick's assistants were among the twenty or so formally dressed people who stood sentry around the periphery of the room. In addition to them, a team of waiters were stationed around the place, one at each end of each table and two at the sides of each outside table.

Autumn sat on Adam's left, in the middle of it all, thinking there seemed to be way too much space between the chairs. In spite of the fact that this was the best meal she'd seen since leaving Claudio's, she didn't feel very hungry, and suspected Maria didn't either. She couldn't help but be curious about their host, though.

It wasn't long before she got a look at him. A bell sounded, and shushing made its way around the room as a line of five men came in through a door behind the raised podium table. The first sported spiky red hair and a fitted leather jacket over a T-shirt. Mick came in right behind him, absent the top hat, with his hair down around his shoulders, and wearing a long, gray furry jacket in an animal print. Autumn couldn't tell if it was faux or real, but decided to give him the benefit of the doubt. Bringing up the rear was a pale guy with smooth skin and dark hair just long enough to curl. He wore charcoal slacks and matching jacket, with a red button-down and silver jewelry, and walked behind a tall, stern-looking black man with chiseled features and a bald head, in black suit and shirt.

Autumn forced herself to look at them before focusing on the man in the middle, who simply had to be their host, because she knew if she settled on him first, she would never be able to tear her eyes away. There was something horrifying about him, and she suspected it wasn't the dramatic way he dressed.

He wore black leather pants, and a silver-studded leather jacket over a black T-shirt with a white image on it she couldn't see. He jingled when he walked, as though there were chains on his boots. His long black hair was cut in shaggy layers. It was his eyes, though, that made Autumn shiver—black and hard, as though he had seen way too much to be impressed by anything.

The men sat. The man in the middle planted his elbows on the table and clasped his fingers below his chin, looking over the audience as Mick had earlier. Autumn expected frightening sounds to come out of his mouth, an animal growl or something high-pitched and evil. To her astonishment, his voice was clear and pleasant, even warm.

"Good evening, friends," he said. "As some of you may already know, I am Freddie Biali, your host. I do this a couple of times a week to get to know as many of you as possible. Like many of you, I too, am a vampire. I know what it means to live without a community, to live in fear of being found out, of people reacting in fear because of what was done to me hundreds of years ago. This is why

I built this place, and now offer it to you as a place to play and network with those of your own kind, and as a place of safety for those of you seeking shelter. Biali House welcomes all.

"However, opening my home to everyone necessitates a few unfortunate rules, which you will find in the booklets in your rooms. They mostly have to do with the dress codes for particular events and areas of the house, etiquette—which is very important—what you may and may not do with house feeders and the feeders of others, what your particular package gets you. If you are staying here for free as a feeder, you must provide the use of your body in some fashion to fellow guests or my staff. If you want to get credit for a service, please see a member of my staff before the transaction takes place. I can't tell you how many people have come crying to me that they didn't get credit for banging some guy in the stairwell when no one knew about it. If that happens to you, it is your problem. I still expect documented payment. Vampires staying for free must provide at least one feeder for use. That means the feeder pays her own tab plus his, which is two uses per week per couple, three uses per week from a triad and vice-versa. Check your jealousy at the door. I don't have time to deal with it. I and my staff put a lot of time and energy into making sure everyone has a good time and remains safe.

"After dinner, we will retire to the Smoking Room, which is exactly what it sounds like. If you simply can't bear to be around the smoke, there is a smoke-free parlor across the hall—and yes, I will be making my way over there as well. In the meantime, we have a wonderful dinner prepared by my kitchen staff for feeders and any vampires who still like to chew. For the rest, there are a lot of delicious feeders on the menu. Please be patient as they make their way around to you."

The crowd had come in through two sets of double doors across the room from Biali's raised table. Through these same doors filed in two lines, mostly women in brightly colored gowns. The men were dressed in suits, but wore no ties, and had the top few buttons of their shirts undone. Each held a small red cloth.

Biali continued speaking as the feeders infiltrated the tables in formation. "There are one hundred and sixty-nine vampire guests here with us tonight," Biali said. "I have provided two hundred feeders. They are heavy producers, so don't be afraid to take as much as you want, even if you see marks on them. They know when they have reached their limit, and will tap either the table or your person when they need to be released. Feel free to make reservations for later if you see someone you really like.

"Those of our guests who are feeders, please—eat. Enjoy our little banquet. You taste much better when you're well fed."

Adam jumped when a beautiful woman in an emerald gown with fiery red hair piled on top of her head put her hand on his shoulder. "Would you care to dine, sir?"

"I just, uh…"

Autumn tapped his arm with the flats of her fingers. "Go on, Adam. For the experience. It's not like you're going to get fat."

He looked around nervously. "I'm just…I haven't eaten at a table for nearly sixty years."

"Well," the woman said with a warm smile. "It's easier than it looks. Mind if I sit on your lap?"

Even Maria had trouble containing her snickers as Adam reluctantly acquiesced and the woman sat gracefully on his lap, then handed him her little cloth. "Will you put this on me? It goes on my shoulders to protect the dress."

Autumn looked around the table. There were already many feeder-women sitting on the laps of vampire men, with red drapes over their shoulders, offering their throats while feeders filled their plates next to them and chatted with other feeders. Vampire women sat on the laps of their male feeders. A few of the same-gender couplings seemed to be busy trying to determine who should sit where, based on body size.

There was a feeder to Autumn's left, a thin young man with pink cheeks who seemed to belong to the well-dressed man sitting next to him. "Have you been here before?" Autumn asked the boy.

The boy nodded. "It gets pretty crazy. There's a reason they have security here. Some of the vampires…all the feeding gets them horny and they'll fuck anything that doesn't move. Or that doesn't move fast enough."

The vampire next to him—a tall, square-jawed man with a practiced salesman's smile and short, neat hair—stopped feeding to turn his head. "Language, Joey. What have I told you?"

"Sorry, sir," the boy said, then shrugged at Autumn when his master went back to the woman on his lap. "It's true, though," he whispered. "Most people don't care, because they know they're here to be used in every way possible and they love the lifestyle of servicing vampires. If they get dragged into a corner on the way to the bathroom, that's fine with them."

"Is it fine with you?" Autumn asked the boy.

"I guess, but he's picky about who touches me, so I could get into a lot of trouble if something happens and he hasn't approved it first. What about you?"

Autumn shrugged. "We're just here to see what happens. We haven't been here before."

The boy nodded. "It's a good place. Just be careful late at night, is all I'm saying."

Chapter Eight

A SURPRISING number of the vampires turned out to be smokers, among them the man with the 1940s haircut. "I could use a little something myself," Adam said to the girls.

Autumn wanted to interact with everyone, but didn't know what to say. People stood close when they talked, touching each other briefly on the arm, exchanging information and affection. Not far away, one of the house feeders stood patiently as a vampire man grasped her chin and turned her head this way and that, scrutinizing her features, then took her arm in one hand and used the other to squeeze her bottom. "Oh my God, Maria, look," Autumn said, unable to keep the enthusiasm from her voice.

Maria nodded. She stood with her elbow propped on her hand. "I know. It's a den of decadence in here," she said disapprovingly.

"Prude," Autumn teased tentatively, watching to see how Maria took it.

Maria gave her a guarded smile that warmed gradually before she looked away.

A man with platinum curls and sparse, hot-pink highlights leaned in. "Isn't it just terrible?" he asked in a deep, silky voice. He was older, with some crinkling around his eyes, but those eyes were a startling shade of blue. "Hi girls, I'm Francois. Frank, really, but Francois is good for business."

The man from the Internet café.

Autumn froze.

"What do you do?" Maria asked while Autumn forced herself to take deep breaths.

"Hairdresser to the stars, baby. I'm one of the best." He bent down toward Maria. "Did you know that having a man who knows what he's doing wash your hair in the shower is one of the most erotic experiences you will ever have?"

"Really?" she asked. "That's so startling I think I need a drink. Do you want anything?" she asked Autumn.

"Sure," Autumn said, narrowing her eyes at the man, who shot her a self-satisfied grin. "Whatever you like."

"I like beer," Maria snapped. "But unlike us, I don't think that's on the menu. I'll find you something girly. Excuse me."

"Wow," Francois said. "She must have had a hard day. You don't think I upset her, do you?"

"Are you stalking me?" Autumn asked incredulously, just as Adam came over.

"What's up?" Adam said. "I'm Adam. These are my girls."

Francois widened his eyes in surprise. "Really? That's… interesting. I'm Francois. It's great to meet you, Adam." He held out his hand. I was just talking to—what's your name, beautiful?"

"Autumn," she said, eyeing him warily. She wondered why he found it so "interesting" that she and Maria were "Adam's girls."

"I was just talking to Autumn here. I hope you don't mind." He smiled quickly.

Adam shrugged. "Not if she doesn't."

"Good," he said, rolling his shoulders and relaxing his face, looking from one of them to the other. "Because I have to tell somebody about the weird thing I saw on the way over here this afternoon. There was a guy standing by the side of the road, right? Playing guitar in his underwear, like that guy in New York, the Naked Cowboy. Have you heard of him? He's been playing his guitar in his underwear for money for about ten years, only he has the body for it. The guy I saw today trying to do that was about fifty years old with a belly the size of a Volkswagen. It was amazing. It made me cringe."

Autumn made a face in spite of herself, intrigued.

Francois looked at her, cocking his head slightly and lowering his lids just a little. He pointed at her. "See? Just like that. That face is how I felt on the inside. You are so cute," he said. "Here, give me a hug. Maybe you can squeeze that image out of my brain."

Autumn smiled and let him put his arms around her, relaxing a little. He kissed her on the side of the head. When she looked over at Adam, she saw him talking to a statuesque black woman with smooth, dark skin.

"Let's do an experiment," Francois said. "Give me your hands like this."

"You didn't answer my question," she insisted. "I saw you today at the Internet café. You looked at my computer."

He let his gaze linger on hers for a moment while locking fingers with her right hand and squeezing. "Yeah?" he said. "I guess you did."

She returned the squeeze absently. "You looked at me."

"I thought you were pretty. Now think of a number from one to ten."

Autumn found herself doing as she was told, then dropped her jaw at him. "You looked at my computer."

"I recognized the site."

"What about the honey bun?" she insisted. "You're a vampire and you bought a honey bun."

He furrowed his brow at her. "How do you know I'm a vampire?"

"Because you sniffed the room when you came in. Like you were looking for someone."

"Habit," he said, with a sheepish smile. "Do you have your number?"

"Why did you buy a honey bun?"

"If you must know, it was for my boy. He has a sweet tooth. Now are you going to let me impress you with my little trick or are you going to interrogate me all night? Hmm?"

"Go ahead," she said.

"Are you thinking of it?"

She nodded.

"You were thinking of…five."

She furrowed her brow and shook her head slowly. "No."

"That wasn't it?" he asked with an exaggerated expression of disappointment.

"No," she repeated.

"Got you to hold my hand though, didn't it?" He let his face open into a wide grin.

Autumn dropped her jaw, liking him against her will. "That's just…" She pulled her hand away, fighting the urge to smile.

He ignored her protests to pull her close, then push her away and plant a kiss on the top of her head. "You're adorable, you know that? Listen, I have to go now, but I hope I'll be seeing you around. Are you guys going to be here long?"

"I don't know," she said, squinting and trying to figure out how she felt about him. "We haven't decided."

He took out a pen and a card, scribbled something on the back. "Here's my room number if you decide you want to hang out." He handed her the card. "Oh, I *am* a vampire, in case you were wondering."

"Yeah," she said, keeping her eyes on him in case he did anything else.

He backed away, held up his hand and waved with his fingers, then blew a kiss.

Maria slid up next to her, holding two drinks. They both watched Francois go. "I think he was trying to get rid of me," she said, handing Autumn an amber liquid. "It's an amaretto sour. You'll like it."

The last sentence sounded more like an order than a prediction, but Autumn wasn't in any mood to notice. She took the cocktail, cold to the touch, surprised a few seconds later to find herself drinking it without noticing. "It's...like dessert."

"Definition of a girly drink," Maria said, nodding in the direction Francois had gone. "That guy is a lot smoother than he looks, by the way. There's something almost familiar about him. I can't put my finger on it."

Autumn shrugged, hoping she was faking nonchalance well. "He's looking for sex. That's what everyone's here for, sex and feeding."

Maria didn't reply right away. When Autumn turned to her, she was pressing her lips together thoughtfully. "What if there are people here looking for something else?" Maria asked. "This would be a perfect breeding ground for illicit activity."

Autumn thrust her head forward and widened her eyes. "Illicit activity? What are you talking about?"

"I don't know, Autumn. But there are bad people in the world. Not everyone is what he seems."

"So admitting he's a vampire isn't enough? What else could he possibly be hiding?"

"I don't know. A lot of these guys are pretty old. They've had a lot of time to do things they don't want people to know about, is all I'm saying. They've had a lot of time to perfect their…game, for lack of a better word. I just don't want to see you get hurt."

"I think you're jealous," Autumn snapped.

Maria wrinkled her brow and hung her head briefly.

"I'm sorry," Autumn said, tearing up, regretting her tone. "I just…I'm sorry."

Maria nodded, blinking rapidly. "It's okay. I knew this was coming, Autumn. I did. You were always so eager when we were together. I knew you were hungry for new experiences. I didn't really expect it to last forever. I just thought we might have some time before you decided to stretch your wings, is all."

Autumn smiled. "I still love you. You're my best friend."

Maria gave her a sad smile. "Not exactly the title I'd hoped for, but I guess it'll have to do." She put her arm around Autumn. "I'll kick that guy's ass if he hurts you."

"He's not going to hurt me. He's a hairdresser."

"Like Sweeney Todd?"

Autumn rolled her eyes at her and sipped her drink. "Sweeney Todd's a barber. Everyone knows barbers are much creepier than hairdressers."

"I hope you're right," Maria said.

Chapter Nine

AFTER DINNER, Adam presented Maria with a new dress he'd bought her in one of the gift shops. It was long and red and went with a favorite pair of shoes she'd brought from home. She held the fabric in her hands and looked at it as though she had no idea what it was. Then she looked back up at him with tears in her eyes. It brought tears to Autumn's eyes too, and she was glad Adam had found a way to make Maria happy.

"I got myself a pair of good shoes too," he said, holding them up for her to see. "I know we can't really afford it, but it should get us into some of the better events. Maybe we can find something fun to do tonight."

Maria nodded frantically, unable to speak, and ran to the bathroom. "Thank you," she sobbed on the way.

"There are methods to make money," Autumn said tentatively when she was gone. She sat at the table, flipping blindly through the laminated book of house events.

Adam raised his eyebrows, looking through the clothes he had laid out on the bed. "Don't you even think about it. I don't want you out of this room by yourself, either.

Do you understand? No going out. Vampires are natural predators and I don't want you getting hurt."

"All they want is to feed and have a little fun, Adam. What's so wrong with that?"

"Do what I say. I want you here when we get back."

She flipped a page and let it fall over. "When are you coming back?"

"I don't know. Could be in half an hour, so you just stay put. Familiarize yourself with what there is to do here or something."

"Yes, massa," she said quietly.

He froze with a black shirt in his hand, and gave her a stern look. "Oh no you don't. Don't pull that 'massa' bullshit on me."

"Or what?"

"Or what, nothing. Just don't."

Autumn sighed. Since dinner she had started to feel a little frustrated and couldn't really account for why. She wondered if it was her encounter with Francois, or whether she felt left out because Adam and Maria were taking a night to themselves.

A few minutes later, Maria came out of the bathroom in her red dress. It was a sleek little number, but Autumn pictured her dancing in a festival in something with ruffles, whooshing her skirt and teasing the boys, wearing huge matching flowers in her hair. She had always envied Maria's dramatic Latina looks. Maria had always said they looked good together, dark and light, buxom and waifish, passionate and...*and what?* Autumn wondered. What had been her counterpart to Maria's boisterous passion? Whatever it was, Autumn thought it must have turned into something else, some lust for life in whatever form it came to her, a Bacchanalian ecstasy, a thirst that rivaled that of any vampire she had ever met.

Adam dressed in a new gray jacket he had bought in one of the on-site stores, wing tips, jeans and a black T-shirt. "Put your hair down, like this," Maria said, sounding almost like her old self, fluffing the hair that already rested on Adam's shoulders. "And you need some gold. We'll have to get you a gold necklace when we have money."

"You girls are going to drive me crazy," he said while reaching around to take down his hair, smiling in spite of his words. It hit his shoulders with a thud. "Better?"

"Much," Maria said. She grinned at Autumn, most likely out of habit, Autumn thought, because the grin disappeared almost as soon as they made eye contact. Maria blinked her eyes quickly and looked away, then forced herself to smile at Adam. "I'm ready. Let's go see what kind of trouble we can find."

"With you in that dress, I think the trouble is probably going to find us," Adam said and held out his arm. Over his shoulder, he added, "Remember what I told you. Stay here. You've already gotten into enough lately."

Autumn nodded and sighed. "I'll be right here," she said miserably. She was glad Maria and Adam were going to have some fun, but her energy level was way too high to be stuck in a room by herself, even a ridiculously elegant one like this.

She stared down at the book. It was a large, black spiral binder with three D-rings to hold plenty of laminated pages. It advertised masked balls, feeder auctions, vampire auctions, mixers, pool parties, cocktail parties, fetish events, concerts and burlesque shows. Guests could purchase packages entitling them to attend particular events provided they were dressed appropriately.

She flipped to the Nonpaying Guests section, which promised "A Host of Events for You As Well." She felt skeptical, but discovered many of the events were open to non-paying guests as long as they could pay the cover and had the right clothes. Plus, there were several bars in the place, and a vampire could always sponsor people he or she liked into an event.

"Wow," she said to herself. "You can get turned on just by looking at this book." One photo in particular reminded her of something that could be used to advertise a Cirque du Soleil performance—a man in white-tie surrounded on either arm by four women in sequined and feathery dresses. The man wore a leopard eye mask and the women wore elaborate bird masks. The photo was taken from a vantage point lower than the subjects. The two women on the ends bent their knees toward each other, showing their thighs through the slits in their dresses.

Autumn wanted to be there. Whatever went on during one of those masked balls, she wanted to see it. She wanted to do it. She flipped to another page, to see images from a fetish ball—a slender young man on an X-frame cross getting flogged, a man holding a whip in both hands at crotch level and giving the camera a penetrating look, a woman standing on the backs of two men posed on all fours, holding reins attached to their bits. She went back to the photo of the man with the whip. Something about the look in his eye held her. She slid down in the chair and reached between her legs to press the seam of her jeans against her labia, undulating middle and index finger, trying to make it hurt just a little.

She almost didn't hear the knock on the door.

Letting her jaw go slack, Autumn groaned louder than her pleasure demanded, just to hear the animal sound of her own voice. When the knock came again, it was more forceful and was accompanied by a man's voice. "Hello? Adam? Autumn? Anyone?"

She froze. It sounded familiar, but she couldn't quite place where she'd heard it before. For a moment, she almost pretended not to be there. Then she decided that would be silly, especially if whomever it was had heard her unrepentant moaning. She blushed. "Co…coming!" she called, which only made her blush harder.

Autumn straightened her hair on the way to the door, combing her fingers through it and snagging a tangle. "Ow!" she muttered, barely working it out before making it across the room, shaking the loose strands from her fingers to the bare hardwood floor. Then she put her hand on the doorknob, took a big breath, sighed and opened the door.

It was Francois, and he had a bottle of Scotch and a boy with straight, longish hair with him. "Hi, Autumn. I thought if you and your friends weren't doing anything, maybe you'd like to share some Dewar's. I just got it on the way here. Oh, this is my boy, Josh. Say hi, Josh."

"Hi," Josh said, sizing her up behind Francois' back.

"Mind if we come in?" Francois asked.

"Uh…sure," Autumn answered, stepping aside. "Adam and Maria are gone right now, though. They'll be back later."

"Do you have plans?"

"Not me. They ditched me to go see what this place is about."

"Then I arrived in the nick of time," he said, spinning around to face her, opening his arms wide. "Would you like a drink?"

"Sure," she said, and went to the minibar to look for cups.

"If you don't like it," Francois said as he set the bottle down on the bar, "I have some mixers in my room."

Autumn shook her head, not at all comfortable with the idea of going back to his room. In light of what she had done with Bill the guitarist in the French Quarter, this struck her as strange.

"No, I think I'll like it," she said, finding a small stack of individually wrapped plastic cups and unwrapping them.

Francois poured without speaking, seemingly content to have her watch him work, and handed her one.

Autumn put her nose into the cup and sniffed. The smell was strong and sharp. She had never been curious about Claudio's whiskeys, but she had been different then. The sip she took burned all the way down and made her cough. That was twice today, she noticed.

"We should probably water that down," Francois said and took it back, going over to the mini fridge and taking out a bottle of water. Autumn marveled at the way he made himself at home. "You know, in my old life, I never would have gotten my own bottle of water. If they'd had bottles of water." He twisted off the cap and poured some into her cup, then handed it back. "Here, try that. Better?"

"Much," she said, glancing at Josh, who had found his way to a chair and claimed it. He leveled his eyes at her and did not blink or smile. "Does he want anything?"

"He doesn't drink until he can behave himself better. He's like a twenty-year-old child."

Josh looked away, grinding his teeth. His whole body seemed tense. Before she could look away from him, he turned his eyes on her. There was something dark there, seething just under the surface, barely under control. She turned away and sipped her drink.

"You know what we need?" Francois asked, wandering away from the bar with a cup of his own in his hand. "Music."

"Oh, it's too bad Adam's not here," Autumn said, suddenly excited. "He could play his saxophone."

"That's not exactly what I meant," he said. "Something softer. Violins, maybe? Hmm?" He turned on his heel and raised his eyebrows suggestively. The gesture reminded her of Claudio.

"Here," he said before she could react, offering her hand. When she gave it to him, he began to hum a waltz she didn't recognize, then raised their hands and spun her, endangering the barely filled cups of whiskey. "See what fun we could have if we had an orchestra in our room?"

She wanted to feel like laughing, but had no idea how to respond to him. And then he was off again, taking long strides toward the bed, then flopping onto the foot and sloshing whiskey up onto his hand. Both Autumn and Josh moved for the paper towels at the same time.

"I'll get it," Josh growled.

"No, no, Josh, let her do it," he said, holding his hand away from his body and grimacing. "Can't you see I did that on purpose to give her an excuse to touch me?"

Josh glared at her for a moment before crossing his arms and standing there.

"Go sit down, boy. And do something about that foul mood before I send you back to our room. You're the one who wanted to come. Remember?"

Josh blinked and nodded, hanging his head a little. "Yes, sir," he said, and returned to his chair, looking off to the side and blinking rapidly.

The exchange caused Autumn's stomach to tighten pleasantly. She remembered how Bill in the French Quarter had spoken sternly to her before having his way, and wondered if this man would be the same—*if* she'd wanted to play with him, which she didn't. He was just a little too smug for her taste, even though he had managed to intrigue her. She handed him the paper towel. "I'm not going to touch you," she said, her voice soft but firm. "You'll just have to do it yourself." She hoped there was a challenge in her eyes.

He looked up at her for a moment, then gave her a surprised smile before taking the paper and dabbing at his wrist. "Clever, clever girl. You know exactly how to keep yourself out of the clutches of a vampire." He patted the mattress beside him. "But come sit with me. I have to know something."

"What?" she asked, and sat.

"Why a lovely, and I'm sure very tasty, girl like you is sitting all alone in her room." He pinched her chin between finger and thumb and guided her eyes toward him. "Have you been a bad girl, Autumn? Are you being punished?"

For a moment, the tight ball in her stomach warmed. For a moment, her lips parted and her breathing deepened. Then she shook her head. "No. It's not like that. Adam doesn't punish."

"I'll bet you wish he did, though," Francois said and turned away, leaning back on his free hand, sipping his drink.

Autumn stared. "What's that supposed to mean?"

Francois shrugged. "Just that a lot of the people who are into vampires have those leanings. Call it a hunch, but I wouldn't be surprised if you had a red *derriere* right now."

"No, I don't," she said, standing up. Technically, it was true, because the belt-marks Bill had left were now blue.

"That surprises me," he said, rising with her, moving deliberately, holding his drink off to the side and standing close to her. "Would you like one now?"

She shook her head hard, to clear it, and whirled to face him. *"What?"* In spite of her bold beginning, she shrank from him.

Without touching her, he lowered his head to whisper in her ear. "I know what to do with naughty girls who have to stay in their rooms, Autumn. I've had decades… and decades…of practice."

She could smell him—a sweet, musky soap, cologne, the hint of maleness. A series of hot chills spread over her back. She could swear she felt every individual hair stand on end. Suddenly, Francois moved away and drank the rest of his Dewar's. "I'll let you think about it," he said. "Enjoy the rest of that. Oh, and…" He strode over and planted a kiss on her lips. "That's to remember me by. Like I said…you know where to find me."

He scooped up his bottle from the table, put down his cup and headed for the door, followed by Josh. Autumn could only watch, dumbfounded, and try not to let her legs shake visibly. She took a step forward as he opened the door and motioned for his boy to go out first, then went out himself, turning at the last moment to flash her a big, fanged smile before closing the door.

Chapter Ten

"I KNOW what to do with naughty girls who have to stay in their rooms, Autumn. I've had decades...and decades...of practice."

Autumn wondered if Francois knew his words would keep her awake that night, touching herself. Bill had simply been desperate to find someone to fill his needs. He would have gone after anyone he thought he could steer back to his room and under his belt. Francois spoke as though only *she* would do.

She felt restless. She needed a walk. Her heart beat quickly at the thought of taking Adam's key from his pants and slipping out the door. She could probably get out without disturbing the others too much. Maria had come back tipsy and Adam seemed to have too much on his mind to notice the strange smells that must have been in the room, including those of whiskey and other males. Or, she thought, maybe he just assumed the smells were from the cleaning staff.

This had been the first night since they had started traveling that Autumn and Maria lay with Adam between them. It saddened her in a way, but she was glad things were out in the open now. At least, most things were. It seemed that every time one thing settled itself, something much more interesting happened.

Very carefully, she sat up, trying not to shake the bed too much. Adam snorted and moved around a little, but didn't roll over. She perched on the edge of the mattress for a moment, listening to their breathing, then stood and began feeling around on the floor for the jeans Adam had worn out that night. It wasn't hard. They smelled like cigarette smoke.

There were two skeleton keys on a ring in the pocket. After a lot of pulling and fingertip pain, she got one of them off and put the other back, then felt around for her own jeans, pulled them on and headed for the door in bare feet. The bed creaked just as she got the key in the lock.

"Autumn..." Adam's voice was rough with sleep.

"I'm just going to the pharmacy," she whispered. "Stomach's upset."

"Want me to come with you?" he asked groggily.

"I'll be fine," she said. "It's not far."

"Be careful..." He was snoring within seconds.

She had never used a skeleton key before and had to crouch over the keyhole for many minutes to get the door to open. She didn't realize how tense the position had made her back until she stood. The knob was a little loose in her hand and the hinges creaked, so she opened it slowly. Maria whimpered and turned over in her sleep. Autumn's heart pounded, partly because she wondered what would happen if the others actually became conscious, and partly because she wondered what would happen if they didn't.

She crept out into the cold hallway, wishing she had thought to bring a jacket. Or socks. *Too late now,* she thought, and shut the creaky door again, tempted to leave it unlocked. What were the chances of someone coming along and trying to get into their room? she wondered, then realized she really had no idea what would likely happen in a place like this. The thought made her shiver.

Finally, she got the door locked and put the key in her pocket, then took a moment to listen, in case Adam or Maria stirred. Hearing nothing, she backed away from the door, feeling very alone in the high-ceilinged hallway. She began to tremble. For a moment, all she wanted was to open the door and rush back in, climb under the covers and stay there, but she turned toward the hallway instead.

It was mostly dark, lit only by electric wall sconces. She stepped carefully, in case the staff had missed sweeping up a stone or something sharp. *This place is full of vampires,* she thought. *Horny vampires on vacation.* This time, her shivers were accompanied by heat between her legs, and she wished she was in a dress, like in the movies.

She rounded a corner and found herself on a short hallway with no rooms, and windows on both sides. She wandered to the right, positioned above a courtyard, with a fountain for a centerpiece. Moonlight shimmered off the water, even as shadowy plants moved in the breeze on either side of the cobbled walk. At first she was alarmed to see movement here and there. Then she realized some of the guests had decided to take moonlit strolls, which had obviously led to other things. She had a pretty decent view of a man pumping a woman lying beneath him, her dress raised to her hips. She wondered which of them was the vampire. Judging by the percentage of vampire men she had seen at dinner, she decided he was.

"Those people are completely scandalous," a man's voice whispered behind her, making her jump. She turned with a hand over her heart to find Francois standing there, grinning. "Scared you?"

"Yes!" she said, and smacked him on the arm. "Are you still stalking me?"

He put his hand over his heart and gave her an exaggerated look of shock. "Who, me?" he asked. "I just have a hard time staying in my room. I'm practically living in this hallway. I haven't slept well since the turn."

"Of the century?"

He laughed. "*No-o-o.* Longer than that, baby. Longer than that. Since about 1788,1789. Around then."

Something about that date struck her as odd, but she couldn't put her finger on it. "Oh," she said. "I thought you were younger, for some reason."

He gave her another look. "You really know how to make a guy feel good about himself. Now if you'll excuse me, I have to go cry in my room."

Autumn laughed, genuinely this time.

"Now she's laughing at me. You really are an evil woman, you know that?" he said. "I don't know if I'm safe around you. Hey, I have an idea. Why don't we go down there and do something to them?"

"Do something to them? Like what?"

He shrugged. "I don't know. Throw some water on them or something."

"We can't do that!"

"Why not? Ooh!" he said, hunching toward her excitedly, touching her arm with the backs of his fingers. "I'll tell you what. I have a water pistol in my car. We can get that, and it may not make them quite as angry as some of the things we could do. What do you say? Do you want a little adventure?"

"Well..." Autumn said. Pranking the courtyard couple sounded like a great idea in theory, but she wasn't sure how it would play out in practice. Besides, it was cold out there.

"Oh, come *on,*" Francois said, turning to look out the window with a mischievous smile. "Live a little."

Autumn followed his gaze. "I wasn't really planning on leaving the building. It's—what time is it, anyway?"

"A great man once wrote that time is an illusion."

"What great man?"

"It doesn't matter. He's dead now. But I'm alive and standing right before you, wanting to take you on the adventure of a lifetime."

"Squirting people with a water gun is the adventure of a lifetime?"

"Well, all great adventures begin with something fun. Come on."

Autumn smiled. It did sound like fun, and she didn't mind being lured into the shadows by a fun, handsome vampire for a session of something that would probably turn into debauchery. Even if he was pompous and annoying. She nodded. "Okay. But I can't be gone long. Adam and Maria are expecting me back."

"It will only take a minute," he said and took her by the hand to pull her back down the hall toward stairs. "They won't know what hit them," he said. "And the water should be nice and cool by now."

Outside, the night air was almost frosty. "Oh, it's cold. And I'm barefoot," she said. "I shouldn't be out here like this." She turned to go back inside, but he put his arm around her shoulders.

"Never fear," he said, and took off his jacket to hold it for her. She looked longingly at the door, but soon acquiesced and allowed him to slip it up over her arms and drape it on her shoulders.

"It's way too big," she said.

"Well, you can't have everything," he teased, and picked her up in his arms, making her squeal. Something about the sudden motion and the feeling of being pressed against his chest made her want him to touch her, made her ignore the pricking on the back of her neck that told her something wasn't quite right.

"What do you drive?" she asked.

"Something really cool," he said, focusing his eyes ahead, no longer smiling. Autumn thought he may be concentrating on finding his car, or on not stepping on something that would cause him to stumble with her, though she had never met a clumsy vampire.

The parking lot was down the hill and across an expanse of grass, which meant he would have to carry her for about a mile. "Are you sure it's worth it to go all that way for a water gun? We could do something else to them if you want." Assuming the water pistol was just a ruse to get her into the shadows to do naughty things with her, she added, "Or…something else, by ourselves."

"It's worth it," he said, ignoring or perhaps unaware of her hint. "Besides, we can't back down now. It would be against the rules, and we've already come all this way."

Something about his insistence spooked her.

"Francois, I…I think I really want to change my mind. I don't want to do this."

That got his attention. "You're not serious," he said, his voice warm again. "Am I frightening you? Here, let me put you down for a moment. Your feet are going to get cold, though."

He let her slide out of his arms. When her bare feet touched the cold pavement, she shivered visibly.

"Aw…come here," he said, and put his arms around her. "I shouldn't have brought you out here like this. Will you ever forgive me?"

"I just don't want to do anything to those people anymore. They're probably gone anyway."

"Perhaps," he said, and grew quiet.

Autumn thought there was something odd about the embrace, and about his sudden change in mood. She knew she should go back inside, but it felt as though he were coiled like a rattler, and that any sudden move or suggestion that betrayed just how alarmed she felt would cause him to strike. The odd thing about the embrace, she realized, was Francois' lack of passion, even though he seemed to be trying to seduce her.

She began to tremble as she realized things really weren't quite right and she was far away from Adam. Just as she was beginning to wonder if she should scream and run for the door, she heard footsteps coming up the walk—two sets, belonging to men, not quite in sync.

"What's up, man?" one of them said to Francois. It was Freddie Biali, carrying a stylish black walking cane, and he had Mick with him. Though his tone was friendly, it carried an undercurrent of something else. It reminded her of the way Claudio had sounded when he thought his feeders might be up to something.

"Mr. Biali, Mick. The lovely Autumn and I are going for a nice walk in the moonlight. It's a perfect night for it."

"In bare feet?" Mick asked, looking at Autumn. "You must be freezing. Here," he said, taking off a red furry coat, similar to the one he had been wearing at dinner. "This one will be warmer."

Autumn looked at Francois regretfully, not wanting to insult him even though she had been ready to run screaming a moment before. She felt glad he moved to reclaim his jacket himself.

When Mick made a subtle movement of his head to call her over, she noticed he was wearing a pair of goggles on top of his woolen hat. She went to him and let him put the coat on her. "There. That has *got* to be better."

"It is. Thank you." Unsure what Biali's and Mick's intentions were, and what Francois' reaction was going to be, she began to tremble harder. She really wanted to go back to her room.

It was Biali's turn to speak. "I hate to be a cock-blocker, man, but there's no taking other people's feeders off premise."

"We were just going for a walk—"

"This place has two courtyards, and both of them have a lot of cover," Biali said. "And this girl is not dressed for walking out here. It's freezing for them."

Francois nodded, and tightened his jaw. "Right," he said, glancing at Autumn. "I guess I didn't think of that. Perhaps we should go inside to the library and talk, yes?"

"Actually," Biali said, "I want a few minutes with her myself. I think I need to clue her in to appropriate feeder behavior."

Autumn's stomach sank to her feet. Her lips parted in surprise. She looked at her bare toes, which seemed much too vulnerable on the pavement, and wondered if the vampires were going to punish her.

"All right," Francois said. "I'll just wait and we can go to the library afterward."

Mick bowed his head and snickered, swiping his lip with his thumb.

Biali shook his head. "I was speaking rhetorically, my friend. I have a few videos in my office I'm going to show her. You won't be seeing her again tonight. You two can hook up tomorrow, *on* premise."

Francois nodded. "I see. Well," he said, turning to Autumn. "Come find me." He then turned briefly to the other men and went back toward the building. The others watched him go. When he was inside, Mick said, "Shady."

"No kidding," Biali said. "Come on. Let's get you inside."

"Am I going to be punished?" she asked as Mick herded her toward the door, barely able to make the words come out through chattering teeth.

"Not by us, if that's what you're worried about," Biali said. "You'll have to take that particular issue up with your vampire. We do want to caution you, though, that not everyone here is on the up and up. You will have people trying to take advantage of you. I don't know what that guy was up to, but it didn't look good. What did he say?"

"He said we were going to his car to get a water gun to play a trick on someone."

Mick looked at Biali, alarmed. "Classic kidnap scenario. Do you know his name?"

"Francois. He says he's a hairdresser."

"We'll check him out," Biali said. "In the meantime, don't let strange vampires lure you out of the building. It isn't safe."

"Yes, sir," Autumn said, moving to open the door. Mick put his hands on her shoulders and kept her in place while Freddie opened it instead.

"You are so cute," Mick said, squeezing her shoulders. "Can I ask you something?"

Autumn nodded, then walked through the open door and turned around. "That vampire you're with—Adam, isn't it?"

She nodded.

"Some of us thought he looked familiar. He's with that group, isn't he? Claudio du Fresne's chamber group?"

The door closed. Autumn felt all the color drain from her face. She wondered if the two vampires could see it in the sparse lighting. "Yes," she said quietly. "He was, but ...we left, and...we didn't have anywhere to go, so we came here."

"Diamond is so going to rub my nose in this one," Mick said. "Plus I'll owe him fifty bucks."

Autumn frowned, confused.

"One of his assistants," Biali explained. "He recognized Adam and genius here told him he was full of shit. Oh well. Live and learn," he said, clapping Mick on the shoulder.

Mick rolled his eyes. "Yeah, yeah."

"I can't say I'm surprised du Fresne's scaring people away," Biali said.

"You know him?" Autumn asked, astonished.

"Know him? I helped get him on his feet in this country. He likes to lay low, doesn't think he needs the community. Don't worry, though. We have a no-snitch policy."

"That's good," she said. "I don't think he's very happy with us right now."

Biali turned to Mick. "Why don't you get her back to her room? I'm going to wander around a while longer and then see about getting something to eat."

Mick nodded to him once.

"Good luck," Biali told Autumn, then left, twirling his cane.

"Come on," Mick said, putting an arm around her. "You're still freezing. What in the world were you doing out in bare feet?"

She shrugged, letting him lead her toward her room. "I couldn't sleep, so I decided to take a walk."

"That's not a good idea to do on your own the first time you come here, not as a feeder. We go to a lot of trouble to make sure our events are safe for everyone involved, but it's a big place. Things can happen in dark hallways."

She shrugged. "I was kind of hoping something would."

Mick did a double-take. "You little minx. I knew there was something about you I liked. And you're making me hungry. I don't suppose you've, um, paid your dues yet, have you?"

"No," Autumn said guiltily.

"Is your vampire up?"

"No, he's sleeping."

"Sneaking out. I tell you what. You come off all sweet and shy like a kitten, but I'll bet there is a *li*-ttle tiger in there somewhere." He touched her nose with a fingertip. "Well, that's too bad. I would really like to taste you."

"You can," she said. "I don't mind."

Mick shook his head. "No. I like to make sure it's all right with everyone involved first."

"I'm not really with him. I'm not his. We're just traveling together as friends."

"Does he feed from you?"

"Not really. It's a long story."

"Well, I'd still better talk to him first. And here you are," he said in front of the door. "My coat, please," he said, holding out his hands.

She began shrugging out of it, but he helped her and put it back on. "I don't feel complete without it. You take care," he said, bending down to kiss the corner of her mouth. "And maybe I'll see you around."

She nodded and watched him go. It took her a while to get the skeleton key to work, but eventually she was inside the room, trying to close the door without creaking it too much.

Chapter Eleven

THE NEXT evening found Autumn, Adam and Maria staring at a royal blue evening gown and white furry mask laid out on the bed. *Please accompany me to our monthly Cat-and-Mouse Ball—Mick,* read the attached card.

"He wants you to go to this ball with him," Adam said.

Autumn had not mentioned the previous night's adventure with Francois, admitting only to meeting Mick after a short walk, and that he had refused to bite her because he couldn't ask Adam's permission. Adam had grunted, but he did seem on the verge of giving her his blessing to go to the ball. For some reason, that felt very important to her.

"I do need to pay my portion of our fee for the week," Autumn said, turning to Maria. "And so do you. It's at least one session with each of us and a third from either, on behalf of Adam."

"I know what the cost is," Maria said crossly. "But I don't have pretty managers and gay hairdressers stalking me. That was really weird, by the way, that thing with that guy Francois."

Autumn's stomach grew hot. She wondered if Maria knew how long she had been out the night before. "He's not gay. He's just…you know how bisexual Claudio is. Vampires are just…like that."

"Whoa!" Adam said. "*I* am not like that. I like girls. Only girls. Always have, always will."

"You're an exception in a lot of ways, Adam," Maria said. "But I don't know. Something about that guy is really creepy."

"Maybe," Autumn said. She did have a point, and Francois had tried awfully hard to get Autumn to his car last night. And Mr. Biali and Mick had both thought he was "shady." Not to mention Francois' lack of an erection. Maybe he'd been trying to kidnap her or something. She wondered why a vampire she had just met would want to kidnap her.

Underground feeder slave market?

She shivered. Whatever his intentions had been, she had suffered a close call and didn't intend to do that again. At least she would be safe at the ball with Mick.

"I guess you'll be all right with him," Adam said, echoing her thoughts. "They've got a vested interest in keeping their customers safe."

When she called the phone number scribbled on the card, Mick picked up immediately, and insisted on speaking to Adam. A few days before, she would have bristled at the two of them behaving like an old-fashioned suitor and father, but after her close call, she enjoyed feeling protected.

* * * *

Mick showed up at six that evening in a tuxedo and ponytail. The only remnants of his previous rock-star attire were eyeliner and black nail polish. He carried a black cat mask in his hand. Adam opened the door.

"Hey, man," Mick said, and offered his hand, held high and at an angle. Adam clasped it.

"Yo," Adam said. "What's up?"

"Just a little bit of fun for this cute little redhead here," Mick said. "I hope it's still all right. I don't want to step on anyone's toes or anything." He glanced briefly at Maria, raising his eyebrows as he did so. Autumn wondered if he could tell what was going on between them. He'd had a long time to learn to read people.

"Nope, no toes," Adam said. "But she is my friend, and I don't want anything to happen to her."

"She'll be safe with me. Which reminds me…" He dug in his pocket and brought out a sapphire blue pendant on a silver chain. "I want you to wear this. It's a panic device, in case we're separated and you need me. Press the jewel and it activates a remote in my pocket. Got that?"

Autumn nodded and turned for him to put it on her, glad for both the extra protection and the extra jewelry. She hadn't brought anything appropriate for a formal event.

Mick took her to dinner in one of the on-site restaurants. Even though she had been used to eating around vampires who weren't partaking, she found it a little unsettling that he was actually sitting with her and watching her eat. His teasing smile didn't help.

"Am I making you nervous?" he asked over his clasped hands.

"A little," she said. "I'm used to vampires being in the room when I eat, but I haven't actually sat down with one like this since…since Claudio took me out when I first met him."

"Claudio. Yeah. The guy who lost my bet for me."

Autumn nodded. "Yeah. I was with him for several years and now—I guess it's not really a good thing to talk about it too much."

"Hey," Mick said. "This is a place of safety. Whatever your reasons for leaving, they're your own. You don't have to justify anything to me. Frankly, I'm glad you did leave him. That means I get something tasty on my plate tonight." He raised his eyebrows several times.

Autumn bowed her head, blushing. "About that," she said. "What's going to happen tonight?"

"Well, here's how our masked balls tend to work. We arrive together, but we don't necessarily stay together, if you know what I mean. It's a way for vampires and feeders alike to release their inhibitions. Some vampires keep their feeders right there with them, and anyone who wants a piece of their action has to approach the vampire. Some turn their feeders loose to do whatever they want. It's important for you to remember, though, that everyone here has the right to say no to anyone else here. We uphold whatever arrangement the vampire and his feeders have, but aside from that, everyone is treated on equal footing."

"Oh," Autumn said, aroused. "I see." She had to force herself not to squirm in the seat, and blushed when she remembered vampires could smell sexual arousal.

"So you like that idea," he said, and took a drink of his wine.

She nodded, keeping her eyes on her plate.

"Good. That's one reason I brought you. I've noticed that girls—and guys, a lot of the time—who wind up in that situation are led astray by their own need for adventure. Am I wrong?"

"No," Autumn said quietly, staring at her plate.

Mick put his hand over hers. Its warmth made her shiver. "Don't worry. You're not in any trouble here. You didn't do anything wrong. But I think it will be a good thing for you to have an adventure that's a lot safer than that. Don't you?"

"Yes," she said more decisively, smiling up at him.

He resumed his hand-bridge position, raising his hand and keeping beats with his outstretched fingers from time to time. "Here's how it's going to work for us. We'll go in together and do a walk-around. That serves two purposes. One, it lets everyone know you're with me. Just another safety precaution. Two, it lets people who may be interested in you get a look, and vice-versa. You can see who's there and who you might like to get a little attention from. Now, these things usually get pretty decadent pretty fast. You're going to see people fucking on the furniture all over the place. It looks very elegant and pretty, but it's just feeding and fucking everywhere. You can stay with me, or wander off, whichever you're more comfortable with. You're under my protection, and I take that very seriously, okay? Just know I'm going to be sampling from the menu pretty heavily. And likewise for you. You can do anything there with anyone you want, except give up too much blood. I actually want the option of having you as my dinner when it's all over. I would prefer you didn't let anyone bite you at all, but I know how tempting it is in the heat of passion. Any questions?"

Autumn shook her head, then stopped. "Oh, wait. Yes. What's the other reason?"

"Other reason for what?"

"What's the other reason you asked me? You said giving me a safe adventure was one of the reasons."

"Oh. My *other* reason," he said, with a wink. "I have a serious thing for redheads."

* * * *

The Cat-and-Mouse Ball was held in a section of the house that Freddie Biali had lived in when it was first built—encompassing dining room, parlor, library, bar and three bedrooms, as well as a long hallway with plenty of nooks and crannies.

Mick assured Autumn that all of the furniture she saw was extremely sturdy.

When they arrived, she noticed immediately that all the "cats," or vampires, were dressed in black semi-formalwear—black-tie tuxedoes for the men and black evening gowns for the few female vampires there, with matching masks. The "mice," or feeders, were dressed in every other color imaginable, with white mouse masks. It looked as though female feeders outnumbered male feeders, but not by as many as male vampires outnumbered female vampires.

Eyes followed Autumn as Mick paraded her slowly around the parlor and through the library. When a blue-eyed man came near to eye her up close and show her his extended fangs, her heart began to pound. For a moment, she thought it might be Francois. Then she noticed his hair was more a sandy brown, and the blue of his eyes was nowhere near as intense.

"It's okay," Mick said, patting her hand as it rested on his arm. "You don't even have to leave my side if you don't want to."

"I'm okay," she said. "This is…exciting."

"That's my girl. But don't feel like you have to be too brave or anything. You're here with me for a reason."

Other eyes looked her over briefly and then turned to scan the next morsel to walk past.

"Would you like a drink?" Mick asked.

Autumn almost said yes. She had discovered she liked the heady feeling of a little alcohol in her system. But she didn't feel exactly safe with all these lecherous vampire eyes checking her out, and that feeling was heady enough. She knew she wasn't hiding behind Mick all night long, and wanted to keep her head on straight.

"No. I think I want to experience this as it is," she said.

"Good choice. I think I'll—"

"Mick, old friend," a female voice purred. Autumn turned to see a glamorous blonde beauty in a black evening dress and black cat mask. She was with a diminutive girl dressed in white, wearing the requisite mouse mask. "This is the girl I told you about. I'm helping her prepare for a life as a feeder. Poor thing doesn't want to go into service as a virgin and I thought you would be the perfect man to help her out with that."

Mick opened his eyes wide. "You mean a literal virgin?"

"A virgin in every way," the woman said. "Perhaps you can find the time to train her in the ways of pleasure?" The woman glanced at Autumn but did not acknowledge her.

Mick cleared his throat. "I would—be delighted to speak with her about it." He looked apologetically at Autumn.

"Don't worry," Autumn said. "I know how weird you vampires can be. I'm going to wander around."

Mick nodded. Relief spread over his face. "I'll catch up with you later," he said, and bent low to kiss her on the cheek.

Autumn nodded and looked at the girl, who stared at her with awe. No one had ever looked at her like that before. She hurried away before the others noticed her blushing and the girl decided she wasn't so cool after all.

It took only seconds to see a tuxedoed man pressing a woman against the wall, her stocking-clad leg wrapped around his through the slit in her dress, her foot missing its shoe. When Autumn realized she was staring, she turned away abruptly, and ran into the solid form of a pale-skinned vampire man with a slight smirk on his full lips. What hair had not been buzzed from his scalp appeared blond. His eyes were dark blue and unflinching.

"Oh," she said, blushing. "Sorry."

"Don't be sorry," he said with a slight German accent, allowing his extended fangs to show as he spoke. "I was admiring your form."

He took an arm in one hand and turned her body. For a moment, she thought he was going to spank her, but he only slid his other hand around the silky fabric of her dress to her bottom, making circles with his entire palm. He groaned, then turned her around and pulled her back against him. She could feel his erection pressing through the fabric of his slacks. "I'm going to fuck you," he whispered in her ear. She caught her breath. "Where everyone can see."

He bunched the fabric of her dress to open the slit on the side and slid his hand beneath it and between her legs. Panicking, she searched the crowd for Mick, but did not see him. A delicious sort of fear began to find its way into her body as the vampire held her tightly with his left arm, using his right hand to pull down her stockings and panties, exposing her tender parts to anyone who cared to look. Several men, vampires and feeders alike, came closer as the German held her on display.

"See all these men?" he whispered. "They want to stick their cocks in you. Just like I want to stick mine in."

Heat and cold. She was aware of heat moving between her legs, spreading its tendrils into her organs and down her limbs, and chills moving over her shoulders and arms, mingling with the heat between her legs to form forbidden, thrilling sensations. Her crotch was not supposed to be naked for all the guests to see at a formal party and she certainly was not supposed to feel this way about it.

A large, dark-haired man who reminded Autumn of a mafia don sauntered over with a fanged grin showing beneath his black mask. His wide frame and thick neck were not usually what she went for, but the intensity in his black, sparkling eyes and the sensuous curve of his lips held her attention. "I would really like to touch this one if you don't mind," he said in a gruff New York accent.

Autumn's heart hammered against her breast bone.

"Be my guest," the German said. "But I fuck her first."

Autumn watched the Italian's heavy-lidded eyes with horrified fascination as he stepped close and covered her breast with his large hand, radiating heat through the thin fabric of her gown. "Nice," he said. "I wouldn't mind tasting her either."

"I'm…I'm Mick's dinner," she managed to say.

"Well, we won't infringe on anyone's dinner," he said. "But a little snack won't hurt anything." He pinched her nipple until it hardened to a little point, making her breathe heavily, then kept his eyes on her face as he slid his hands beneath the bunched fabric in the German's hands to press his hot palms against her stomach. "I'm thinking of that nice little pussy that's dripping just inches below my hands, and how I could be so very happy sliding my dick in there."

Autumn swallowed, wondering if it would be possible to back out at this point, thrilling with the thought that it may not be. She ached for the Italian to touch her pussy instead of only talking about it, even as vampires drifted closer and closer, giving her long looks, unconcerned about their fangs showing. They reminded her of sharks.

Giving the Italian a smug look, the German picked her up in his arms, just as Francois had the night before, and carried her around the nearest couch. No one had yet claimed it. He lay her there and disposed of her stockings, panties and shoes, dropping them in a pile by the couch, lowering his head to sniff the scent between her legs. "She's ready," the Italian said impatiently.

"I found her," the German countered, flicking his tongue out to tease her swollen labia. "I'll fuck her the way I want."

Autumn arched her back involuntarily, and looked around. Some of the guests watched her with a cool curiosity; some seemed to be calculating the chances of getting in on the action. Others were involved in their own flirting games and didn't seem to notice. She hadn't realized things would be so public. The thought of being on display for so many vampires as a man she had never seen before did what he wanted both appalled and excited her.

The German's tongue teased the crease of her groin and played outside the periphery of her pussy, making her ache to have him return to her labia and clit. Very slowly, he began to tease her clitoris with feathery touches, moving down and around the sensitive folds of skin, skipping over her opening to lap up the juices dripping out of her, stretching his eyes to watch her reactions.

She lifted her hips toward him, wanting more, no longer caring who gave it to her or who saw. A thin man with dark hair and chiseled features under his mask stood on the other side of the couch and unzipped his pants, not even trying to hide the fact that he was staring at her naked pussy as he brought out his erection. "Fuck her," he hissed. "I want to see you fuck her."

The German ran the flat of his tongue from the spot just above her anus up over her quivering opening and through the labia, then raised up to look at her.

"Time to give the people what they want," he growled and opened his pants.

His erection was thick and meaty. He grabbed it and jerked the uncircumcised foreskin up over the head and back again a few times, letting the pre-come drip onto Autumn's inner thigh. Then he mounted her and pushed at her opening.

Being surrounded by so many watching strangers made her clench her muscles, making it difficult for the vampire to enter her gently. One forceful thrust of his hips, however, got him past the barrier and made her gasp.

"Oh my God," she whispered.

"Fuck her," the thin dark-haired man hissed, pumping at his erection with his hand.

The German rocked his hips against her, pushing at her softer parts with his pubic bone as he stretched her wide. "That's it," he whispered back. "Take it. Take that cock."

He lay his body out against hers and pumped her harder. She smelled the hint of soap against the side of his neck. It occurred to her in a flash that he wouldn't be clean for long, before she could no longer think for the stranger's relentless pounding. She turned her head to the side to escape the smell of him and the sight of the dark-haired man masturbating and cheering him on. The Italian stood by looking down at her calmly, waiting without urgency. It sent a prickle up her spine that made her want him.

The German lowered his head and licked the side of her neck with just enough pressure to make her shiver. Her body cried out for the bite, even as she squirmed under him. She thought of Mick, and how he was expecting to feed from her later. The thought sent waves of heat through her belly and down between her legs. She slid her arms under the vampire's jacket, feeling the muscles in his back working as he rutted into her, listening as he grunted with each thrust. His lips went slack. He threw back his head, tensed and filled her with his juices.

The Italian cocked his head and smiled. "My turn," he said.

Breathing heavily, the German scraped the points of his teeth along her neck, then pulled out. Someone handed her a small ornate towel, but before she could clean herself, the Italian was straddling her chest and tapping the slick head of his cock against her lips.

"Take it, baby, come on," he urged, so she opened her mouth and let him slide it in, doing her best not to gag.

A woman's voice said, "Clean it up."

Autumn felt a tongue lapping the German's juices from between her legs and it was almost all she could do to concentrate on the cock that was in her mouth. She couldn't see who was between her legs, couldn't tell if the mouth belonged to a male or a female, though she did feel fairly confident it was a feeder.

She had not yet had an orgasm, and felt the tension ebbing and flowing through her body. The ministrations between her legs ceased before the Italian vampire's cock became hard enough to suit him and before he moved off her to settle between her legs and push his way into her with a satisfied sigh.

"This…feels nice," he said, smiling. With a few quick thrusts of his hips, he was inside her up to the hilt, grinding against her, bringing her even closer to climax. She stretched her arms over her head and someone grabbed her wrists. When she looked up, she saw it was the young-looking Indian vampire she had seen when she and the others had first arrived. He held her firmly, but not forcefully. The tips of his fangs were visible.

Somewhere nearby, a woman gave rhythmic whimpers and whines. Autumn imagined someone was pumping into the woman the way the Italian vampire was pumping into her. Autumn moaned, louder than she had thought she would. It seemed to encourage the vampire, who increased the force of his thrusting and began to kiss her throat. Before she could think of what to do, he began probing the flesh with the tip of his tongue. She opened her mouth and cried out as his teeth pierced her flesh.

He fucked her furiously while drawing from the wounds, vibrating her throat with his groans. Her eyes and mouth fluttered open, as they always did, her body well aware it was in the jaws of a predator. For a moment, she panicked, trying to pull her arms away from the Indian and struggle out from under the Italian. Each of them had witnessed the panic of feeders, however. For some, it was simply nothing to be concerned about. For others, it was a turn-on. They pressed closer around the couch. The Indian vampire held her tighter.

Autumn let herself go, allowed her body to ride the sensations of strange men touching her, to spin out of control, tighten and release. The Italian raised his head and licked the blood from his lips, boring his gaze into hers as he pounded his cock into her repeatedly. Her orgasm ripped through her like a beast. She threw her head back and cried out as though in pain, then collapsed beneath him, accepting his come as he filled her and rested his head briefly on her shoulder.

A moment later, he looked up at her. "Thank you," he said, and got up. The Indian vampire moved toward her, unbuttoning his pants, but she shook her head.

"I think I want to walk around for a while," she said, cleaning up with the towel someone had handed her earlier. "It isn't every day I get to go to a vampire ball."

The Indian nodded and turned away, finding his path blocked by a grinning girl in a pink gown and mouse mask. He immediately led her to a round table near a set of bookshelves, bent her over and raised her gown to reveal a set of eager, round ass cheeks and ready pussy. He obliged, and Autumn realized she was staring again.

The Italian chuckled. "It's difficult not to be enthralled your first time. But I'm breaking a sacred rule by making small talk. If you will excuse me," he said, bowed and left.

Autumn watched him go as she picked up her shoes, leaving the panties and stockings where they lay, thinking about how strange this whole experience was turning out to be. She felt very glad Mick had brought her, though, and she walked around, allowing the sights and sounds of people fucking on tables, couches and against walls to excite her all over again. The sensation of having strange men inside of her, not to mention being bitten by a man she had never met before and would likely never see again, one who did what he wanted with her even though she wasn't especially attracted to him, drove the warmth back to the spot between her legs. The knowledge that all she had to do was make herself look available and someone would fuck her made the sensation that much more intense.

Just as she was considering what she wanted to do next, she heard the sounds of two men breaking the sacred rule—only they weren't making small talk. They were arguing.

About *her.*

Chapter Twelve

THE CONVERSATION was brief, and came to her from the other side of a wall just as she padded near with shoes in hand. The first voice was a man's she didn't recognize. The second was Mick's.

"What kind of organization are we if we don't look out for the interests of alpha vampires?" the strange voice asked. "We have to tell du Fresne where they are."

The words made her dizzy. She stopped and put her free hand over her heart.

"You know the policy of this place," Mick said evenly, then lowered his voice. "And this is not the proper venue for this discussion."

"Understood," the other man said after a moment. There was another pause before he emerged from around the wall, meeting Autumn's gaze as he passed, bowing his head briefly before hurrying away.

Autumn stared after him, wondering if maybe she had done something wrong by leaving Claudio with Adam and Maria, broken some sort of sacred trust between vampire and feeder. She looked at the scarlet rug on the hardwood floor, feeling dizzy.

Mick came around the wall, pressing his lips together, looking only slightly surprised to find her there.

"Does he want to tell Claudio?" she asked, unable to keep the panic out of her voice. "I don't want to go back."

"It's okay," Mick said, and took her in his arms. "We don't do that here. My assistant is young yet, and in the process of starting his own family. He'll make a good alpha someday, but for now, he's not confident about his ability to hold things together. So he's identifying a little too closely with Mr. du Fresne in this situation. That's all."

Autumn nodded her head against him. There was something calming about his smell, which reminded her oddly of tea leaves.

"Are you having a good time?" he asked, pushing her away to look at her. "Looks like you've had some action."

She blushed, and tried to hide the shoes behind her back, then smiled and nodded.

"Well, I'll tell you what. I've been to millions of these things and I've got plenty of assistants to take care of things, plus my trusty cell phone. Why don't we go somewhere a little more private, where you can make good on that promise of dinner? I'm starving."

The thought of the beautiful vampire sinking his fangs into her made her shiver, not to mention blush all over again, in spite of what she had just been doing on the couch with strange men. "Okay," she said and took his arm.

* * * *

Mick took her to the library and let her stand in the middle of the room gawking at the twenty-foot high shelves as he loosened his tie and pulled the band from his hair. There was a movable ladder that could slide around the room, and a loft accessible by the next hallway up. Several couches positioned at odd angles, yet somewhat facing the center of the room, sat empty.

"Usually, this is a great room for socializing," he said. "People are here at all hours of the day, making out, talking, whatever. It's like a coffee shop for vampires. Tonight it's empty because there are too many parties going on." He smiled at her and came over, looking at the bite on her neck, which she knew would be closed in a few hours.

"He didn't take much," she said. "I told him I was your dinner."

Mick nodded. "I didn't think he had. Are you okay with this?"

She giggled. "I've just been to an orgy."

"Yeah, but you would be surprised how many people can handle orgies, who can't handle intimate human contact. Vampires and feeders alike. I don't have that problem," he said, moving her hair out of the way to run his finger over the contours of her neck. "It's amazing what happens when you become a vampire. The throat becomes so sexualized. It's instinct. For a regular man, it's what, tits and ass? Maybe a leg. But for vampires, it's tits, ass, leg and throat—not necessarily in that order. You have a very sexy throat."

"Thank you," she said.

He pulled away. "Would you care for a drink?"

She shook her head, and looked up at him, head cocked forward demurely, eyes wide. "No. I want tonight to be real. Whatever happens."

"Oh yeah," he said. "I forgot."

He went to a cabinet in the corner of the room and opened it. He took out one of the red feeder bibs she had seen at dinner the other night, then motioned with his head for her to sit on one of the couches, where he joined her.

"I've been looking forward to this all night," he said, putting it on her like a necklace when she sat with him. "Really and truly. There. Now we won't spill a drop."

When she turned back to him, she could see the slight bulge in his top lip that meant his fangs were extended. She had always found that attractive on the vampires at Claudio's estate, and it was extremely hot on Mick.

In spite of the pounding of her heart, she relaxed as he guided her against the back of the couch, giving her a smile devoid of urgency. It set her at ease. He put his hand on her jaw and gently moved her to face him, then placed a gentle kiss on her lips.

"I want this to be good for you," he said. His voice was deep and smooth. "I don't want to scare you."

She looked away.

"What is it?"

She bit her lip. "I know this sounds kind of weird, but… I'm glad you feel that way. It makes me feel good about you, but…I kind of like it when guys are scary."

"Oh really?" he asked, amused. "Well, I think I can manage that too. Do you want me to go all psycho vamp on you and growl like a beast, like this?" He nuzzled her neck forcefully and nipped at her, making growling sounds. "And this?" he asked, then went for the other side of her neck.

The points of his teeth tickled. She giggled. "Not exactly."

He raised up and looked down at her. "Autumn," he said suddenly, in a firm voice.

She blinked up at him.

"It's time to give me what I want."

His tone sent shivers all over her body. "Yes, sir," she said automatically, then blushed and bowed her head.

He kept his face stoic as he used some force to position her head where he wanted it and pressed his fangs into her quickly, somewhat painfully. She clutched at him, but without the panic she had felt on the couch with the stranger.

She closed her eyes as she felt the hard shafts of his fangs retracting against the torn skin, and the rhythmic sucking from the wounds, thinking about his warm saliva touching her skin and entering her. His hand moved down her body and tugged at the hem of her gown, finding the bare flesh of her thigh. She wound her fingers in his long hair.

He drank for many moments, breathing against her skin, blindly exploring with his hand, pressing against her. In spite of the fact that she had already been fucked by two vampires tonight, she felt desperate for him to take her. She whimpered loudly, hoping he would read it as a sign to do anything he wanted. It seemed to fuel his need and make his movements more urgent, but he did not take his mouth from her throat.

He drank for a long time, lulling her with his rhythm. When he finally raised his head and dabbed the wounds clean with the tip of his tongue, she felt pleasantly warm and mellow. "One of the best things you can do for yourself is let a vampire—well, one who knows what he's doing, anyway—sink his teeth into you. That was really good. Are you up for something more?"

She nodded. He lowered his head to kiss her. "That's my girl," he said, and brushed his lips against hers before plundering her mouth with his tongue.

He undressed her so deftly, touching and murmuring to her all the while, that she hardly noticed it was happening—unzipping the gown and sliding his hands over her back, then pulling the fabric off her shoulders so he could kiss the skin beneath. Before long, she was nude and waiting beneath him as he pressed the head of his erection against her opening.

This felt so different from everything she had experienced with the strange men she had met the past few days. He seemed so much more present, able to hold her with his eyes. Autumn could tell those eyes were looking at her—*really* looking at her—taking stock of her reactions, keeping track of her. It felt as though every movement of his hips, every thrust, was carefully calculated to create in her a specific sensation, to draw from her a particular reaction.

She reached for him with her hips and moaned as he accepted her gift, pressing deeper and deeper inside, taking her more fully than she had been taken in a long time. Slowly, she tensed again toward orgasm. Slowly, the sensation spilled over her. He rocked against her for a long time, letting her float, before finally smiling down at her. "How was that?" he asked. "Was that nice?"

She nodded.

"Do you want me to really fuck you now?"

Surprised, she nodded again.

"Okay," he said. "Hold on."

Mick gritted his teeth, narrowed his eyes and began pounding her without mercy, making her gasp and wonder if it had been such a good idea to agree to being fucked hard by a vampire. Chills gathered at the base of her spine and spread up her back. Each thrust hurt deep inside of her and battered the tender flesh between her legs.

And she loved it.

He came quickly after that, throwing his head back and letting out a long, slow breath. "Whew," he said. "Sorry. I haven't had any in a few days. But I will make it up to you next time. Promise."

"Next time?"

He nodded. "If you and Adam aren't really a thing, then I thought maybe we could spend some time together. I'm in the market for a new feeder, and I like the way you taste."

Autumn blinked at him. Playing around had been fun, but the thought of belonging to another vampire—or to anyone—at the moment, chilled her. She pulled away and sat up. Mick looked surprised but held up his hands. "No pressure. We can keep it low key if you want."

She looked at him. He was so hot, and so beautiful and so everything she liked in a man. But Claudio had been all of that as well. "I, uh…it's just too soon. I just got out of a relationship."

"Right. Well, I won't push you into anything you don't want to do. Just know the offer stands." He smiled and opened his arms. "Come here. I didn't mean to freak you out."

She looked at him, unsure what she wanted to do. He wiggled his fingers and nodded once. "It's okay. It's just holding. I thought girls liked that sort of thing."

Autumn smiled and returned to him, relaxing into the post-bite warmth for a long time. Mick nibbled again before helping her dress and taking her back to her room, where he thanked Adam and Maria for allowing him to spend time with her.

* * * *

She slept deeply that night, and was taken completely by surprise when Freddie Biali woke them up early the next morning and announced they had to leave, unless they wanted to find themselves face-to-face with a very irritable Claudio du Fresne.

Chapter Thirteen

AUTUMN AND Maria huddled together like frightened children while Biali stood in the middle of the bedroom and explained the situation to Adam. "One of Mick's assistants feels that our policy of not informing on our guests is somehow wrong," he said. "He will be dealt with. It's come to my attention that Mr. du Fresne is about an hour away from here. I wanted to give you guys the option of clearing out if you don't want to talk to him, which I see is a distinct possibility."

Autumn and Maria looked at each other, then moved quickly to begin packing.

"No," Adam said. "I'm not running."

Autumn whirled around to look at him, open-mouthed.

Maria advanced on him. "What do you mean, you're not running? You may be a vampire, but he can take *us* back. Do you know what he'll do to us for running away?"

"He's not going to do anything to you. But I'm not tucking tail and running like a…runaway slave." He turned back to Biali, who gave an appreciative frown and nodded in surprise. "Which one told him we were here?"

Biali shook his head. "That isn't important. Believe me, he's going to wish he hadn't."

Autumn felt dizzy. She put out her hand and lumbered toward the bed. Maria noticed suddenly and moved to help her, but Autumn was already sitting. Maria sat next to her and put an arm around her. "We'll be okay," she said.

Adam nodded. "Thanks for giving us the heads up," he said to Biali.

"You can meet with him in my office if you want," Biali said. "I don't think he'll start anything. I know the guy, and he may make a few demands, but I don't foresee a security problem. All the same, security will be there."

Adam turned to the others. "I'll handle it," he said. "You two can stay in here—"

Before he could finish, Autumn was on her feet. "No," she said. "I don't want to run anymore either."

"Autumn," Maria said gently. "You're scared to death of him. Look at you. You're shaking like a leaf."

"I don't care. If we keep hiding from what scares us, we'll always be chased. We'll always have to run. We'll just tell Claudio we're breaking up with him. He's let people go before."

Maria's eyes grew wide. She nodded. "Tell him…right. That's what we'll do. Well, I'm not going to be the only coward hiding in my room. I guess."

"Okay, then," Adam said, turning back to Biali. "Give us a minute to put on clothes and I guess you can show us to your office."

* * * *

Freddie Biali's office was full of books about music and pop culture. It created the distinct impression that, had all the books been in their places, the shelves would have been packed tight. As it was, little gaps dotted them here and there where other books leaned in. Little piles of books covered flat surfaces. In one corner, there was a large console stereo and a shelf of vinyl albums. The only truly contemporary-looking thing in the room was the pristine flat computer screen on his desk.

He allowed them to take it all in. "If you understand the music, then you understand the culture," he said to Adam. "I know you appreciate that. It's important for us to understand the culture as it changes. We have to fit in."

Adam nodded. "This is all kind of new to me. I've been with Claudio since I was changed and we sort of lived in our own little world."

"I can guarantee you, he's kept up with things," Biali said, pointing up at him. "He's a success story. That's how I know things are going to run smoothly today. He's not going to jeopardize the world he's created to have a tantrum about you three. But he is a man with an ego and he will want to confront you to your face. We'll see what happens." He went over to a liquor cabinet. "Anyone want a drink?"

Autumn liked the sound of that. She nodded. "Yes, please."

Biali smiled. "Case of nerves?"

"Yes, sir," Autumn said.

"I guess I'll have something too," Adam said.

"You?" Biali asked Maria.

She shook her head and looked down. "I feel kind of sick as it is."

Biali studied her for a moment, then took down a glass and filled it from a bottle of water on the desk. Then he took it to her. "It'll be all right. Nothing's happening to you in my place. I'm in control here. Not Claudio."

She nodded and smiled at him, accepting the water. Autumn watched her without making eye contact. Biali soon brought Autumn a strong-smelling, fizzy drink. "Hope you like bourbon," he said. "It's pretty much all I have."

Autumn smiled gratefully. "Thanks," she said, and discovered it smelled much stronger than it tasted, but it made the butterflies in her stomach stop fluttering quite so much. Nervousness made her drink quickly, so she was nearly finished with it by the time there was a knock at the door.

"Come in!" Biali called.

A large, bald vampire in a suit stuck his head in the door. "A Claudio du Fresne here to see you, sir."

"Send him in."

Biali set his drink on a coaster at the corner of his desk and faced the door. Autumn looked up and had to hold her drink with both hands to keep it from shaking. Maria pressed near her. Adam crossed his arms over his chest.

Claudio stepped quickly into the room with his lips pressed tight. He wore all black—black slacks with a thin, shiny belt; a black button-down shirt, open at the collar; black wingtips. Even one of his silver rings had a black stone.

Autumn swallowed. She had not really thought about Claudio since leaving, except to worry he may find them and take them back to his country estate in Georgia. The penalty for running away was a severe whipping, even more severe than the whippings he usually gave. She was startled to find herself thinking he was still the most beautiful man she had ever seen, with his deep, black eyes, large nose and heavy jaw. Except for a few stray, uncontrollable curls at his jaw that came from a somewhat layered cut, he kept his dark hair shoulder-length and straight, allowing it to curl under at the ends. Since he had been in his mid-forties when he was turned, a touch of gray showed at his temples.

She cringed under his gaze.

When Claudio's eyes fell on Adam, Adam uncrossed his arms and squared his shoulders. Biali, the shortest man in the room, placed himself between Claudio and the others and took his hand, smiling. "Claudio, old friend. How *are* you?"

Claudio gave Biali a stiff smile. "Suffering the pain of the betrayed, as you may imagine," he replied, returning his gaze to Adam. His French accent, still pretty thick even after all his decades in the U.S., made Autumn study his features more closely. She wondered if leaving had been such a good idea. Had they really betrayed the man who had rescued each of them from their respective Hells?

Adam looked down briefly and shifted on his feet.

"What are you going to do, Claudio?" Biali asked soothingly.

Claudio looked at him, lowered his eyelids slowly in an expression that sent shivers up Autumn's spine, and smiled more warmly. "I want to speak with them, to determine if this is what they want. To let them know it is not too late to return to me."

He looked at Adam, who sighed and shook his head. "We talked about this before. I don't want to return. I don't want to live the way you live."

Claudio moved slowly around Biali and stood in front of Adam, who was a couple inches taller. "You will have to keep slaves," he said. "There is no other way."

"Don't call them that."

"Feeders, then. You will have to catch them, and you will have to discipline them."

"I just don't see it that way."

Claudio turned toward Autumn and Maria. "Do you truly want to leave?"

"What would happen if we came back?" Autumn asked. Maria elbowed her.

"You know what would happen, my dear. I make no apologies for punishing my…feeders. But don't base your decision only on fear."

"I'm not going back," Maria said. "I want to live without vampires."

Claudio worked his jaw. "I see. And you, Autumn?"

"I don't know…" she said quietly, wiping a tear from her eye. "I'm…confused."

Claudio softened his expression and moved toward her. Biali put his arm around Claudio's shoulders and stopped him. "Why don't we give her some time to think about it?" he said.

"But of course," Claudio answered. "It is simply that my family is very important to me. I don't like to leave them out here in the world like strays."

"That's understandable, man. I don't blame you. But they're not exactly children."

"No," Claudio said. "Of course not." He turned back to Adam. "How will you make money?"

"When we first met, you told me I could be a god with my playing. If that's true, I ought to be able to scratch out some kind of living."

Claudio nodded. "Making something with music is difficult. When I came to this country I had my family's fortune, and it was still difficult to create a world to live in."

"I'll manage," Adam said, rubbing his face.

"I knew this day would come," Claudio said. "But you should not run away. Let me help you. I know many people, many vampires, who will welcome you. I do not wish to rob you of your freedom."

Adam nodded. "Thank you. Maybe we should talk," he said with a shrug. "Man to man."

Seeing Claudio's gentler, more charming side made Autumn homesick. Everything she had been telling herself these past few months, everything Maria had told her, seemed like a dream. She felt sick, and wondered if it was anxiety or her body responding to Claudio's nearness. She had belonged to him mind, body and soul. He had made love to her, fed from her, taken care of her, as well as frightened her and punished her. And now, after thinking of him as a monster who would rip away her freedom and enslave her once more, she wanted to rush over and fling herself into his arms.

She had to escape and think for a while.

"Excuse me," she muttered and headed for the door. Claudio turned as she neared him. She was afraid he would touch her. If he touched her, she didn't stand a chance. When he looked at her, she stopped in her tracks and gazed up at him, lips open and eyes wide.

"I've missed you," he said. "My shy little flower."

Autumn swallowed. "Maestro," she said quietly.

He dropped his lids and smiled. When he reached to touch her face, she ducked out of the way and fled to the door. Then she turned around. "I'm going for a walk," she said. "I…I have to think. I'll be back for breakfast."

Maria took a few steps forward, but Autumn put up her hand. "I need to be alone for a while," she said, then went out the door and pushed past the large, surprised-looking vampire standing guard. She jogged down the hall, just in case anyone decided to follow her.

Autumn walked without thinking. The important thing was just to keep moving. She tried to push the sick feeling down and out of her stomach, caused from being torn between freedom and family. She wondered if she had really wanted to leave, or if she had simply been letting Maria make her decisions for her.

Yet, if she went back with Claudio, she would get the whipping of her life. She also knew he was right, and that she shouldn't let fear be the deciding factor. At the moment, though, she just wanted some peace from the thoughts that threatened to pull her in eight directions at once.

It wasn't long before she found herself outside. The brochure had mentioned several areas to walk, beyond the parking lot—gardens, wooded paths and even a meadow for horseback riding. She thought some time in a garden would be ideal and followed the cobbled path from the house toward the lots. The path snaked around the outside of the concrete and veered into a wooded area.

She felt better already, even though it was chilly out. She decided to warm up by walking fast.

A few people loaded belongings into vehicles as she walked past. She wondered if any of them were the vampires themselves, or if they made the feeders do all the work, as Claudio had. The thought brought tears to her eyes. "Damn," she muttered.

On the other side of a sparse growth of trees was a green area crisscrossed with the same cobbled path she had been following. In the distance there was a fountain, much larger than the one in the courtyard she had seen the other night. She wondered how cold the water was and wandered absently in that direction. Beyond that, a couple walked hand-in-hand.

The water was painfully cold, but she enjoyed feeling it on her hand in the brisk air. It seemed dangerous. For someone who had been Claudio's "shy little flower," she thought, she had certainly made a lot of decisions in her life based on following danger around, as opposed to avoiding it.

Letting Claudio take her had been a good example. Yet that had put an end to much of her exploration, as life with Claudio had consisted mainly of doing chores around his estate and being available for him and the other vampires who had lived there. Of course, it had been exciting at first, but life had eventually settled into a routine, broken only by the occasional outing with Claudio or one of the others. Of course, the whole "family," as Claudio enjoyed calling his group of vampires and feeders, would attend the vampires' chamber performances. It had not turned out to be the sort of dangerous life she had imagined. Or else she had simply grown accustomed to it.

She watched the water for a long time, trying not to think about Claudio. Part of her wanted to rush back into Freddie Biali's office, throw herself at Claudio's feet and beg him to forgive her for running away. Part of her was prepared to take any punishment he deemed necessary to teach her a lesson. But she knew if she did, she would sit in safety and mourn all of the unknown things that could have been if she had only kept going. In the play of the clear water in the fountain, Autumn saw that her path lay ahead, not behind.

The hand over her mouth took her by surprise. Too startled to scream, she flailed in her captor's grip, but was on her back before she could make contact with fists or nails. She saw Francois' burning blue eyes above her, then the flash of his fangs before he forced her head to the side and pierced her flesh, holding her still and drinking until she lost the will to fight.

Chapter Fourteen

AUTUMN KNEW something was very wrong. Francois was taking her somewhere. She tried to hold her eyes open, but indeterminate colors swam in front of her.

Eventually, she was deposited roughly on a seat of some kind. A door slammed. She tried to make out what her senses were telling her but faded out of consciousness, and had to remember all over again that she was somewhere with Francois when she came to seconds later. Another door slammed. A motor started and the thing she lay on began to vibrate. She had barely enough time to register the fact that she was in a vehicle before she passed out.

* * * *

Autumn's eyes were too heavy to open. Someone was talking to her, squeezing her face painfully. "Wake up, you little bitch," a man's voice said. There were traces of a French accent mixed in with the West Coast that she now realized must have been carefully cultivated. She opened her eyes to see Francois' angry face above her.

He straddled her as she sprawled on the back seat of a van. He was so heavy. She looked around. The van was long and windowless.

Kidnap van, she thought. Then she saw Josh, standing a few feet away with a handheld video recorder pointed at her. "What are you doing?" she asked.

François grabbed her face again and made her look at him. She tried to push his hands away but couldn't find her own. It took her a moment to realize they were tied above her head and fastened to a bar bolted to the side of the van. Panicking, she thrashed around under him, trying to get her legs free so she could kick. He slid down to sit on her thighs, then ripped open her jeans, tearing the buttonhole and tearing denim from zipper, then forced them down and popped her hard on the bare hip. The pain jolted her from her stupor. She cried out.

"Don't make me hurt you," he said, revealing the tips of his fangs as he forced the jeans off her. When she kicked him, he went over to one of the van's bucket seats, picked up a leather strap and whipped her with it.

"Stop!" she begged. "Please stop!"

He paused and stared down at her, flaring his nostrils and flexing his jaw. Autumn became aroused, in spite of the circumstances.

Francois smiled. "I knew one of Claudio's would respond to this," he said and held up the strap. "His taste hasn't changed much in two hundred years."

"Claudio?" she asked, confused. "I'm not with Claudio anymore. Who *are* you?"

He tossed the implement aside and began unbuttoning his slacks. "Then why is he coming for you? Are you a runaway?"

The question made her heart pound even more. "I thought you were gay," she said quietly, staring at the bulge in his pants.

Francois laughed and rubbed the slick head of his erection against her opening, making her gasp unwillingly. "This isn't about sex, honey. It's about revenge, and revenge makes me horny. There are things that happen with us grownups that you won't understand. Claudio took something from me a long time ago. So now I'm going to take something from him."

With that, he pushed inside of her, pumped her a few times and turned to Josh. "Bring it closer," he said.

Josh did as he was told. Autumn looked up, and found him glaring at her while pointing the lens at his master.

"Hello, Claude-Michel. It's been a long time, lover. I see you're still picking cute, innocent-looking little *flowers*." He gave Autumn another couple of hard pumps. "I wonder how much this one can take, hmm? Let's find out together, yes?"

Autumn tried to keep herself from becoming aroused so she could keep a clear head, but it wasn't working. The whole thing felt like a game. Francois was just another random man controlling the situation and taking what he wanted. She couldn't convince her body otherwise.

Francois bent his head down to look at her, with a strange little smile around teeth that were almost bared. "Oh, yes," he breathed as he fucked her. "You've been trained for this, trained to fear punishment and to take what vampires want to give you. I may just have to keep you."

She tried to listen, to gain clues about what he wanted and figure out how to escape, but the warm sensations between her legs were becoming stronger with every thrust. She cried out as he pounded her savagely, partly out of shock and partly from the surprising pleasure building in her body. It wasn't long before she stopped trying to figure it out, stopped trying to resist what he was forcing her to feel, and simply surrendered once again to the sensation of being taken.

She climaxed painfully, throwing her head back and thrashing beneath Francois, who paused and watched with an amused expression on his face.

"Very nice," he said, when she had finished, and began rocking his hips against her. "How did Claudio do it, *cherie*? Hmm? Does he still speak softly to his victims to make them think he is seducing them? I don't need to do that, because I don't care if you love me. Claudio has such a need to be loved by people he thinks are beneath him. He wants to be a god. I don't care if you love me or not, so I don't have to seduce you. I get to just *fuck* you."

Autumn gasped. She closed her eyes and concentrated on how it felt to be pounded by this strange vampire who had kidnapped her and taken against her will and given her one of the most powerful orgasms of her life. She wondered, what else he was going to do to her. Would she belong to him now? Would he punish her for whatever Claudio had done to him?

Francois pulled out, smiling as he rose to his knees and pumped his erection until he came. His thick juices sprayed over Autumn's shirt and bare midriff. She watched his face. Her fear had returned.

"What are you going to do with me?" she asked.

"I'm going to teach Claudio the consequences of his actions," Francois replied, dismounting her and accepting a tissue from Josh, who now held the video camera with one hand. "Unfortunately, you are the one who will have to bear the brunt of the lesson." He turned to the camera as he cleaned himself. "I hope you enjoy the first of my series, 'What's Happening to Autumn?' Stay tuned for the next episode. It's going to be even more interesting." To Josh, he said, "That's enough for now. I'll send it to him later tonight."

Autumn was silent, glad the orgasm had calmed her.

"And clean up that mess," Francois said, waving vaguely in Autumn's direction before heading for the front of the van.

Josh stepped forward and panned the length of her body with the camera, then turned it off and put it in the bucket seat with the leather strap. He tore some paper towels from a roll on the floor and began cleaning her roughly. "He doesn't want you, you know. He's just doing this to piss off that other guy."

"I don't want him to want me," Autumn whispered.

"Good," Josh said, tossing the paper towels into a nearby waste can. "He doesn't even *like* girls."

"Yes, it's Francois Villaforte," Francois said into his cell. "I wanted to let you know I can be there in an hour with the girl. I have tried her and she is very nice. ... No, no one can feed from her yet. I'm afraid I will have to insist. I fed heavily from her this morning. But whoever wants to fuck her is welcome, as long as they don't mind being recorded. ... We'll see you then."

Autumn's heart began to pound furiously. "What's he talking about?" she asked Josh.

"There's going to be a party. Some vampires he knows like to fuck random girls who are brought in for a gangbang. They're going to love you, because you're not exactly willing."

If she wasn't willing, Autumn wondered, why did the thought of being thrown to a pack of hungry vampires send tendrils of heat into her tender areas?

"Can I have my jeans back?" she asked.

"Maybe," Josh said and put his hand between her legs. She gasped and arched her back. "Francois," he called. "Can I fuck her?"

"Later," Francois replied. "At the moment, I want you up here with me. Untie her and tell her yes, she may dress."

Josh stood and gave her a smirk. "Don't make any trouble," he said. "My master will hurt you if you do, believe me."

Autumn held still as Josh untied her wrists and took the rope with him. When he had joined Francois in the front of the van, she pulled her jeans back on and looked around for her shoes, but couldn't find them.

Chapter Fifteen

FRANCOIS TOOK Autumn to a shotgun house in a row of other shotgun houses. The paint, which had grayed with age, was peeling. The porch sagged. There was a dead tree in the middle of the yard.

He parked in front of the house and turned off the van, then walked to the back, where Autumn had remained. She cringed away from him. He had a hairbrush in his hand. "I'm not going to hurt you," he said, sitting down. "I just want you to look presentable. Now turn around."

She did as he said, and tried not to listen to her heart pounding as he began to brush her hair, simultaneously smoothing it with his free hand. "What's going to happen to me?" she asked.

"You're going to be fucked. Really fucked. Do what you're told, or I will beat you to within an inch of your life when I get you out of there. Do you understand me?"

Autumn nodded and bowed her head, trying not to tremble and trying not to let his words arouse her. She knew she shouldn't let herself sink down into this feeling, because then she would lose the will to escape, but she couldn't help it. It was so warm, and so dark and comfortable.

When Francois finished with her hair, he stood up and pulled her off the seat, turning her face and scrutinizing her. "It will have to do," he said, then took her hand and tugged her along behind him. "Come on."

She followed meekly, feeling awkward holding his hand, very aware of Josh and his camera bringing up the rear. She tried to hold her broken fly together with her free hand. Her scalp prickled with fear. She felt cold.

The men sat around the front room watching porn on an old television. There were five of them, all dressed in leather jackets and biker boots. It struck Autumn as odd that there wasn't a tattoo among them, even though she knew that vampires couldn't keep tattoos. She didn't have long to follow that line of thought, however, because one of the men, with a long platinum-colored Mohawk and deep-set eyes, got up and sauntered over to her, chewing a toothpick. The chains on his clothing rattled as he moved.

Autumn shrank away.

"What, is this one a virgin?" the man asked.

"Not by a long shot," Francois said.

"Hm. Too bad," the vampire said and tossed the toothpick on the floor. He grabbed the hem of Autumn's T-shirt and started to pull it over her head. It was too much for her. She pulled away. Several of the men stirred in their seats, but all deferred to a tall, strange-looking man with long dark hair. By the time he reached her, however, Mohawk guy had forced the shirt over her head. The tall man pressed himself against her from behind as Mohawk guy sucked on her nipples, grazing her flesh with the points of his fangs from time to time.

Autumn's body trembled all over with fear and desire.

"That's it," the man behind her said. His voice was deep, and vibrated into her body as he spoke. She leaned into him, partly because his holding made her feel anchored, and partly because the man in front of her was so very aggressive. She cried out and flailed in panic as he pulled her broken jeans over her hips.

The man behind her held her tighter. "Shh..." he said. "Easy."

He lifted her a little when the other man had her jeans below her knees, and took her feet off the ground so Mohawk guy could remove the jeans from her body. He put his arms around her as she looked around at the others.

Mohawk guy kicked an ottoman into the middle of the room. "I get her first," he said.

"Of course," the tall one replied, relinquishing his hold when the other man pulled her away by the upper arms. Mohawk guy took her and bent her over the ottoman. There was snickering among the two of the men still seated. The dark-haired one made a show of rubbing his crotch when she looked over at him. He made a biting gesture at her, showing his fangs. The third, a guy with a head full of blond, squiggly curls, simply watched. It was difficult to look away.

Francois took a seat on the couch next to one of the men while Josh positioned himself in front of Autumn just as the Mohawk guy shoved his cock into Autumn from behind. It was sudden and it hurt. She made a face and cried out a little, looking into the camera, wondering if Adam and Maria—and Claudio—realized she was missing.

"Oh, fuck me! Fuck *me!*" the Mohawk guy said, thrusting harder. Autumn grasped the edge of the ottoman and tried not to look around. She didn't know what to think or what to feel. She knew she should be very alarmed, and she was. At the same time, it seemed natural that she should be here, cringing in front of six frightening vampire men, waiting for them to sink their cocks and their fangs into her.

"Fuck her," someone growled, low in his throat.

Mohawk guy grabbed her hair and pulled back her head, slapping his balls against her and groaning. She wanted to close her eyes, but couldn't. The other three, who hadn't made a move toward her, were much better looking, she thought. The one who had rubbed his crotch had a long, chiseled face and large nose, with his dark hair in messy spikes. He looked to be in his mid- to late twenties. The one sitting next to him looked to be the same age, with reddish hair way below his shoulders. He kept leaning in to whisper to the first, making him laugh. The one with blond curls looked about ten years older. There was a mesmerizing calm about him that Autumn found intriguing.

"Yes! Yes!" Mohawk guy growled as he fucked her deeply, pressing her hips against the ottoman, pulling back hard on her hair and making her screw up her face.

"Give it to her, Manny," the long-haired man said. "I want to see her scream in ecstasy."

The guy with spiked hair pressed his forehead against his hand and shook his head, trying not to laugh.

Autumn wasn't sure if they were laughing at her. They had every right, she supposed. How had she gotten herself into this?

Manny the Mohawk guy tensed and pulled back so hard she had to straighten her arms and push herself up. She cried out, but doubted that was what the other vampire had meant. The next moment, as if reading her mind, he seemed to agree.

"No, no, no. Let me show you how it's done," he said, getting up.

Manny pulled out of her and returned to his chair to collapse, shiny with sweat, pulling a handkerchief from his pocket to clean his cock. Autumn slid back on her haunches and looked up at the long-haired man, who had taken off his jacket to reveal a tight-fitting gray sweater. All traces of mirth had gone from his face as he approached gracefully, lowering himself on his haunches across the ottoman from her. She watched him curiously as he touched her cheek with the backs of his fingers.

"How are you doing, sweetheart?" he asked. "Are you doing okay?"

She nodded, because she suspected that was what he wanted.

"Give me your hand," he said softly.

Autumn found the sound of his voice, and the way he held her gaze, calming. She put her hand in his and stood when he indicated subtly with his touch that it was what he wanted her to do. He pulled her to him. "You're so beautiful," he said. "Will someone move that thing out of the way?"

His friend with spiked hair obliged, and he lay Autumn down on the floor. She didn't mind being naked for him. His voice was so soothing, she forgot they were surrounded by a roomful of men and that one of them had a video camera.

He lay on top of her and brushed his lips over her face, letting his hair curtain around her. "So beautiful." he murmured.

"Oh come on, Tee," Manny said. "Cut the romantic bullshit and just fuck her already."

"Don't listen to him," Tee said to Autumn, before raising his head. "I'll fuck *you,* if that's what you want, Manny."

"Fucking Christ on a stick," Manny murmured, and got up. "I'm getting a beer."

Tee looked back down at Autumn and put his hand on her breast, teasing the nipple with his long fingers, then moving his hand down her body, teasing the folds of skin between her legs. "You like that?" he asked.

Autumn nodded, partly because it was true and partly because she wanted to make this beautiful vampire happy. He played with her for a while, then opened his pants, making the chains there jingle. He parted his lips as he became excited, rubbing the slick head of his erection against her, making her wetter.

"Easy," he said, sliding it in, stretching her.

His body undulated against hers as he fucked her, in and up against her clit, tightening and releasing until she couldn't help but raise her hips to him. "I wish I could taste you," he said. "I want to taste you."

He flicked his tongue against her neck. She wanted him to sink his fangs into her, but knew she had been tapped enough by Francois, and was afraid of passing out again, or worse. So she raised her head to watch the vampire's pale hips rock as he took her, studied his face as he closed his eyes and moaned in climax, felt him throb between her legs and release his juices into her.

When it was over, he opened his eyes and smiled, then dipped his head and kissed her, before standing up. His friend threw a towel at her. "Clean him off," he told her.

Autumn looked around, wondering what was expected of her. Tee smiled at his friend. The quiet man with blond curls sighed and rolled his eyes. The tall man with long hair who had first approached her stood nearby with his feet apart and hands clasped in front of him. Francois leaned against the door frame and smirked. Manny stood in the other doorway and pulled on his Mohawk with one hand, while holding a can of Pabst in the other.

"I don't believe you fuckers," he said, putting down the beer and taking off his belt, moving quickly across the room and striking Autumn hard across the shoulders. "Fucking do what you're told!" he said.

She squealed and scuttled away, clutching the towel to her chest.

"Ma-a-anny," Tee sing-songed, putting his hand on Autumn's head. "Don't be so mean. Can't you see she's confused?"

"Yeah, well, let me *un*-confuse her," he said, taking a couple of long strides toward her.

Tee's friend stood up and got in his way, pressing the back of his arm against Manny's chest. "I'll handle this," he said. "You've had your turn. Go sit down."

Manny stared at him, then put his beer to his lips and drank aggressively.

"Give him the belt, Manny," the tall man said. "We want to have a little fun, not destroy the poor child."

Manny turned and looked over his shoulder, then thrust the belt into the spike-haired man's chest. The other man took it and watched Manny throw himself back into his chair, spilling some of his beer on his chest, then turned to Autumn.

"It's time to do what you're told, little girl," Tee's friend said. "Or *I'll* be the one to use this."

She nodded and turned to Tee, cleaning him with shaky hands, putting a corner of the towel between her own legs.

"Good girl," Tee's friend said, and sat down again. "Now come over here and get me hard."

She crawled to him on her knees and opened the button on his pants. Her hands shook too badly to force it through the tight buttonhole, so he took over and did it for her, taking out his cock, which was impressively thick even before forming a full erection. Keeping the belt looped in one hand, he pulled it out and offered it to her.

Autumn wrapped her fingers around it and took the head in her mouth. The vampire hadn't showered in a few hours at least, and his taste was pleasantly pungent. He grinned down at her, showing off his fangs. "I so want to eat you," he said. "Oh well."

She looked up at him. He was a good-looking guy, the only one here besides the tall quiet man with long hair who was actually her type, although they were all beautiful in their own way. Except for Manny the Mohawk guy.

He was strange-looking and too scary, and she didn't like him at all.

The vampire's erection filled out in her hand and dripped onto her tongue. He moved his hips back and forth, and put his free hand against the side of her head, holding one end of the belt loosely at his side, letting the other end trail the ground.

Autumn wanted to please him for saving her from Manny, because he was beautiful, and because she was surrounded and more than a little afraid. So when he put both his hands against her head and held her there, bringing her repeatedly down on his swollen cock, and finally spilling deep into her mouth and dribbling down her throat, she did her best not to gag too much.

"Beautiful," the tall man with long dark hair said. By the time he got around to mounting her right there on the floor, Autumn had started to zone out. She allowed the rhythm of the vampires' rutting to lull her, slowing her heart rate and not caring very much what was to happen after this. This was big. She knew that. For all practical purposes, Francois owned her now as surely as Claudio had before. But at least she had known that Claudio cared about her. Francois, she thought, was a monster.

And these men could be no better, in spite of the fact that they kept Manny under control. Yet she wouldn't have chosen to be anywhere else than in a room full of horny, gang-banging vampires.

The tall man threw his head back and groaned loudly, throbbing into her, showing his fully extended fangs, filling her with even more hot vampire semen. Autumn could swear she felt it burning inside of her, binding her to these men, and to this life.

When the tall man got up and zipped his pants, Autumn sat up, suddenly self-conscious. She sat on her haunches to hide the wet slit between her legs, and tried to cover herself with her hands, feeling their eyes on her.

"That was nice," Tee said appreciatively, flicking his long hair and turning to the quiet man with dark blond curls. "What about you, Malcolm? Don't you want to try her out?"

For a wiry guy, Malcolm took up a lot of space in his chair. He sat with his legs apart, elbows on the chair arms, pressing fingertips against fingertips, watching intently. "Of course I do," he said, unfolding himself and standing slowly, looking at Autumn. "I just want a little bit of a different arrangement," he said in a low, rumbling voice.

Chapter Sixteen

MALCOLM TOOK his gaze from Autumn and looked up at Francois, who said, "You understand I fed from her deeply, yes? You can't feed again without making her ill."

Malcolm shook his head. "I already ate. But I don't like the camera. And I don't need a bunch of guys looking at my junk when I'm trying to work my magic, if you know what I mean. I want a little privacy. I brought some music too. That's all. I just want to fuck her in private."

Francois thought about it, then shrugged. "I don't see why not," he said. "I have enough footage for what I need to do."

His agreement made Autumn shiver with dread. Being at the mercy of several men wasn't the best of all possible situations, but at least she felt more out in the open here. If Malcolm turned out to be particularly cruel, who would save her from him?

"There's a spare room in the back," Tee said.

Malcolm nodded, then returned to his chair for the little stereo sitting next to it, which Autumn hadn't noticed before.

"Come on," he said, offering his hand.

Again, she felt as though she didn't quite know what to do. She was afraid to go with him, but she knew enough about vampires to understand that, if she refused, she would be punished. Francois had made that clear enough.

Hesitantly, she put her hand in his. He did not pull her roughly to him as she'd expected. Instead, he raised his hand and steadied her as she stood. As soon as she'd begun looking at him gratefully, however, he grabbed her upper arm and tugged her from the room, like a child about to get a spanking. Her heart raced. She wanted to cry.

The back room was small and sparse, built off the side of the kitchen. It had a slanted ceiling, a twin bed and an empty nightstand. Autumn huddled near the door as Malcolm searched for something, found the latch and locked them in, then set up the stereo on the nightstand, and inserted his music player.

Autumn didn't recognize the music he put on. It was grand and dark, with hard rhythms and no words.

"Why did you want…?" she began, but he put up his fingers while adjusting the volume. When he finished with it, he looked up at her and motioned with his head for her to come to him. Swallowing, she took a few timid steps in his direction, squealing when he grabbed her and threw her on the bed, pinning her to the mattress with his weight, clamping his hand painfully over her mouth. She could feel her eyes widen in fear.

"I'm going to tell you something," he said. "Something important. And you are going to listen and do exactly what I say, with no deviation. Do you understand me?"

She nodded frantically, wondering why he was laying down the law like this when she had tried very hard to be obedient tonight, even after Manny had gone bonkers.

"I'm going to take my hand away. You're going to be completely obedient, or you're going to feel my belt on your ass. Is that understood?"

She nodded.

"Good," he said and took his hand away, cocking his head to watch her, studying her face. "Let me hear you say it."

"Yes, sir," she said.

"Good girl," he answered, and covered her mouth in a rough kiss, searching her with his tongue, groaning. The bed creaked as he ground his denim-clad crotch into her naked one, hurting her with the seam, and the huge, hard bulge. He moved from the kiss to her neck. She flinched at the sensation of his tongue on her flesh.

"Don't worry," he said. "I'm not going to bite you. I do want to talk to you, though." The last sentence was barely a whisper.

She turned to look at him, surprised, but found his hand back over her mouth as soon as she opened it to ask him what he wanted to talk to her about.

"I told you to fucking shut up," he said loudly.

His tone made her eyes fill with tears. She nodded.

"Don't talk," he whispered, more gently, grinding into her and making the springs squeak as he talked. "They can hear you, and they may be suspicious of me taking you back here. Now, listen very carefully. I know Claudio. He put out a bulletin that one of his feeders had been stolen—"

"I'm not his feeder anymore," she whispered.

"Runaway?" he asked, with a hard edge to his voice.

She blinked and swallowed, then nodded. "But he caught up with us, and it was okay. Francois wants revenge on him for something. The video's to send to Claudio."

Malcolm nodded. "Claudio filled me in on some of the shit Francois is capable of. You're in a bad situation, so here's the plan. I'm going to offer to buy you off of him, but if that doesn't work, we need to be able to track you. So," he said, pulling a small black cylinder from the pocket of his jacket. "I'm going to tag you."

"Will it hurt?"

Malcolm nodded. "Just a little sting, but you'll be okay. Now hold still."

He pressed it into the back of her neck, under her hair. The pinching sensation caused her to whimper. He smiled and put it back into his pocket. "See there? No sweat."

She nodded. "Is that it?"

"Well," he said, letting his face take on a slightly more lecherous look. "I brought you in here to have my way with you, so that's what I'm going to have to do if I don't want to blow the plan."

She nodded.

He lowered his lids and gave her a mischievous half-smile as he lifted his hips and unbuckled his belt. The jingle of the metal made Autumn's scalp go cold, but she reminded herself she wasn't about to be punished. This man was here to help her, even though he didn't seem to mind taking her in the process.

Malcolm slid into her easily, but only because she was slick with the juices of other men. "Whew!" he said. "Tight. I really wouldn't mind taking you home myself," he said, working his hips. "You'd definitely be better off with me than with that weirdo in there."

Autumn nodded, gasping as he increased the intensity of his thrusting.

"Yeah, you *respond,* don't you?" he said. "I like that."

She kept her eyes on his, even though she was tempted to stare at the fangs growing in his mouth. A vampire man's fangs affected her the way a pair of large breasts affected both vampire and non-vampire men alike—they drew her eyes. She was helpless to ignore them. And they excited her beyond belief.

She liked Malcolm and wanted him to bite her. He wasn't like the others here, and he certainly wasn't like Francois. He seemed kind, yet no-nonsense. The next thing he said further convinced her of that.

"I saw how you reacted when I unbuckled my belt. I don't think what happened in there was your only experience with a belt—was it?"

Autumn stared at him, not sure she wanted to answer that kind of a question. He thrust his cock in hard to help her make up her mind. "Just because I have a job to do doesn't mean I won't wear you out with it. Now answer me."

"No, sir."

"See there? Obedient and respectful. That's a good combination. Now what happens if I spank you anyway?"

Autumn's stomach went hot. When he pulled out, she reached for him reflexively.

He smiled down at her. "Already can't get enough, huh? Come over here." Malcolm sat on the edge of the mattress and patted his thighs. "Don't worry," he said. "This isn't punishment—but it will be if you don't come over here."

Autumn sat up and crawled toward him, eyes down, expecting him to grab her suddenly and force her across his knee. But he only put his hand on her and guided her over. "Let's see how you take a spanking," he said, and brought his hand down on her bottom, making her whimper.

"Very good," he said, rubbing the skin. "Let's see if you can keep it up."

Malcolm continued to spank her, bringing his hand down several times, harder and harder, making her eyes water, then gently caressing the inflamed flesh, occasionally pinching it. She became wetter at his hands than she had all night, thrilling at the danger in his voice and the firmness of his hands. She wondered how old he was, how long he had been handling feeders—or women in general, for that matter. She liked the warm leather smell of his jacket.

She wondered, briefly, what it would be like to belong to him.

As if reading her mind, he told her. "You'd get a lot of these if you were mine. I love spanking asses. My girls get a lot of attention in this department."

"Your…girls?" she asked, barely able to get that last word out as his hand came down again.

"Mm-hm. I have three. I think one is ready to go find greener pastures, though, so there will be an opening soon. Speaking of openings…" He slid a couple fingers inside of her, making her gasp. "You're so easy," he said. "You always react, even after having your pussy pounded by those animals out there."

"I'm just…sensitive."

"I like sensitive," he said. "And I like a girl who knows her place with me. Of course, I can always teach that to her if there are any questions."

"How?" she asked.

"I'm serious as a heart attack about using this belt. If my girls don't do what they're supposed to do, they feel it on their ass, and I don't play when it comes to that. They feel it, and they feel it hard."

Autumn parted her lips and took several deep breaths.

"Man, oh man," he said. "That made you even wetter. You like a man who makes his women do what they're supposed to, don't you?"

"I guess so."

"Well, let me assure you, I do. I'm not an abusive dick-head, though. My girls are happy. I keep them well fucked and I'm an affectionate guy when you get to know me.

Here," he said, and helped her off his lap. "Sit there, on the bed."

He pulled out his erection and offered it to her. It tasted of her own tart juices. "That's it," he said, when she moved the ring of her lips down the shaft. He was a good size—big enough to stretch her pussy, but not so big he had trouble fitting it in. He put his fingers in her hair and looked down at her with a smile. She liked his face. She tried really hard to take him deep into her throat without gagging much.

"I could teach you how to do that really well," he said. "But for now I think I just want to have that tight little ass of yours."

Autumn's eyes widened.

"I know Claudio enough to know that he fucked you in the ass," Malcolm said. "So don't look so surprised. Turn around."

She got up on the mattress on all fours, looking around at him as he reached into his jacket pocket for a small bottle of lube, for which she felt extremely grateful. "Always prepared," he said, and lathered up a couple of fingers.

Her heart hammered against her chest as he pressed a finger against her tight opening. "Relax," he said. "I don't want to hurt you."

With his other hand, he slipped a couple of fingers into her pussy, working them in and out as he pressed at her anus. The sensations confused her. It was impossible to enjoy pleasure in one opening while guarding another, so she began to relax. His fingers rubbing the lube around her anus began to feel good. She began to want them inside her. He seemed to sense that, and slipped one in.

Even through all of her excitement, it felt too big. It hurt, but he obviously wasn't going to stop.

"It's okay, baby. Just relax. Shh-shh…"

She gasped when he slipped two fingers inside, massaging her, getting her to loosen up. The pleasure-pain was so intense, she began to tremble all over. When she felt the head of his erection press against her, she felt faint. She had never liked this with Claudio, and it had always hurt. It had always been something she'd endured because he didn't give her any choice.

Apparently, she thought, all men except for Adam were the same on that score.

She cried out when he slipped in the head, but he held her hips firmly and nudged at her, not forcing it in, but pushing just a little. "Relax," he said. "Let me in, baby. Let me in. It's okay."

Autumn began to cry. Partly from the pain, partly from desire, and partly because she hadn't expected anyone here to speak to her kindly. But there was another reason too. She felt homesick. She wasn't sure whether she wanted to go back with Claudio to the estate or continue with Adam, but she did know that her place was not with any of these men here tonight.

Chapter Seventeen

WHEN MALCOLM was finished with her, he warned her not to say a word about what they had talked about before he'd fucked her. He resumed his stoic expression. Then he turned off the music and gathered his stereo.

Autumn couldn't help but try to hide her nudity as best she could, even though every single man in the room had seen her naked and getting fucked, and most of them had fucked her.

Malcolm sought out Francois immediately and went to him while Manny grabbed her from behind and growled in her ear, nudging his newly erect cock between her thighs. She watched Francois helplessly because she didn't want to look at Malcolm, didn't want them to see that she now put her hope in him. She wanted to pretend he was just another horny vampire who had had his way with her tonight.

"I need to speak with you," Malcolm said to Francois. "It doesn't have to be in private. I'm in the market for another girl, and this one's…whew! She's tight in every hole. I'll give you five hundred for her."

Autumn snapped her gaze up at him as though this was news to her. She let all the horror of one man offering another man money for her show on her face.

"Five hundred?" Francois said.

Malcolm nodded.

"She's worth at least a thousand."

Malcolm looked back at her, blew air out of his lips and said, "No, she isn't. But I like her. So I'll give you seven hundred. Final offer."

"Are you getting this, Josh?"

"Yes sir," Josh said.

"All right. I'll sell her to you for seven hundred. I don't want to know where you're taking her though, or what you're going to do with her."

"Oh, that last part's easy," Malcolm said. "I'm gonna fuck her some more. And if she doesn't behave, I'm gonna beat her ass."

He reached into his jacket for his wallet, and pulled out several fifties.

"Did you come here tonight to do this?" Francois asked.

"Like I said, I'm in the market. You find some awesome feeders in the most unlikely places. Besides, buying and selling slaves is kind of a fetish of mine." He put his wallet away and looked back. "Get dressed, sunshine. We've got to go."

"Hey!" Manny said. "You ain't taking her nowhere."

"I just bought her. She's mine. Now get your fucking hands off her before I feed them to you, and let her get dressed."

Autumn scrambled away from him at the first opportunity and got dressed quickly, letting herself shoot all of the worried glances at Malcolm that she wanted to. She really didn't know whether he would decide to keep her once he got her out of here, and she believed him when he said he'd beat her ass if she didn't do what he told her.

She dressed with shaking hands, partly for that reason and partly because she was afraid the others would smell a rat.

They didn't, though, and it wasn't long before he had her outside and was showing her how to sit on his motorcycle and putting a helmet on her head. She turned and looked at Francois standing on the porch watching her go, and hoped that it was possible for a vampire to rot in hell.

* * * *

Malcolm found a department store and took her in to buy her a couple pairs of jeans, a few T-shirts and a pair of sneakers. She tried them on quietly, feeling that the last few days had just been kind of…off, admitting to herself that she hoped this vampire wasn't going to try to keep her, and that she had made a few mistakes in striking out on her own. She didn't really know what they were, though.

Breaking up with Maria?

No, she thought. As much as she hated to hurt her, she had always considered Maria more of a best friend than a lover, and should never have let the relationship become anything more.

Leaving Claudio's estate?

She didn't think that was it, either. Autumn had spent her whole life imprisoned in one kind of cage or another. Claudio provided a wonderful home for his feeders, she thought, but it didn't provide for much exploration of the world, and she had needed that.

Sleeping around?

That didn't seem to be it, either. She had been with several men up until meeting Francois, almost on her own terms, and that had never happened before. It had always been like this.

"Maybe there's a reason for that," she murmured to herself while Malcolm moved around their hotel room, putting away his jacket and bag.

"What's that?" he asked.

She looked up at him. "I don't want you to keep me."

"Why not? Do you want to be with Claudio?"

She shook her head. "No. He was always much too scary. I think he's going to let me stay with Adam."

"Adam. The one who stole you."

"He didn't steal me. I went with him willingly."

"Autumn, let me make one thing perfectly clear. I—and most other vampires—don't think feeders have that kind of right. I'm sorry, and I know it's very un-PC, but if you were mine, and you ran away like that, I'd whip you so hard you wouldn't sit down for a week. I'm not exaggerating. This Adam—he stole you. You're property, and I wouldn't let myself forget that."

Autumn nodded. "Yes, sir." She couldn't help but say it.

"Now my job is to take you back to Claudio. If he decides he doesn't want you, I may consider taking you myself, if he's willing to let me have you."

In that moment, faced with losing Adam, she realized she wanted him more than anything. "But I want to be with Adam."

"Do you think he wants to be with you now? They filled me in on what happened—the relationship with… what's her name?"

"Maria."

"Right, Maria. The endless fucking. You've been running wild. I've noticed that when a feeder acts like that, she doesn't want her freedom. She wants to be reined in. Maybe Claudio was too much for you. I know he can be pretty harsh. Maybe I can too, but I'm not quite as old-school as he is. I have beat my share of asses, though, and I think that's what you need."

At some point, without realizing it, Autumn had sat on the edge of the bed, head down. His words rang true. "What does it mean?"

"Don't worry," he said. "This mess will sort itself out, as all messes do. I think you'll still be with a vampire, but we'll just have to see which one. Crap! I forgot to call." He reached into his jacket and grabbed his cell.

Autumn nodded, humiliated by her lack of self-knowledge, when she had prided herself on knowing everything. She listened half-heartedly to his end of the conversation. "Hey…yeah, I have her. She's all right. A little used and abused…I'll tell you about it when I see you…day or two. Hey, do you mind if I have a little fun with her while I have her?"

Owned. She would always be owned.

Autumn waited for tears, but they never came. Instead, a warm feeling spread her over her body. No matter who she wound up with, she felt as though she were going home. Malcolm was her savior, and she would do her best to please him while in his care.

He hung up and looked at her. "Well," he said. "Looks like you're mine for the next twenty-four hours or so. You hungry?"

Her stomach growled. Malcolm laughed. "Guess that means yes. Pizza good?"

After telling him what she liked, he told her to go relax in the tub, and he would wait for it. She sat in the hot water gratefully, feeling at last that she didn't have to worry, that everything would indeed work itself out in the best possible way.

Autumn hadn't realized she was dozing until she opened her eyes and looked up at Malcolm, who was leaning in the doorway with his arms crossed, smiling at her.

"Dinner's here. But you're going to have to play a little game for it," he said, and sauntered back into the bedroom.

Game? What game?

Autumn was out of the tub like a shot, drying her hair like mad and toweling off just enough so she wouldn't drip on the floor. She found Malcolm sitting in the chair with the lamp on the floor and the open pizza box next to him on the table. He held a slice in one hand and his erection in the other. Across the room, she froze and stared at him open-mouthed.

He grinned, letting his fangs show. "I never said you wouldn't have to work for your dinner."

In that moment, Autumn wasn't entirely sure she didn't want to belong to this man. She crossed the room and settled between his legs, taking him in her hand and running her tongue up the underside of his erection, watching him shudder. He shook his head.

"Nice."

She inhaled the warm, meaty smell of him, dabbing the tip of her tongue on the tip of his cock, collecting the slick, salty juice there. He groaned deep in his throat. His grip on the pizza went slack. Grinning to herself, Autumn reached for it, but he caught her arm.

"Naughty, naughty girl," he said, standing up, towering over her with her arm in his hand, looking down at her. For a moment, she was worried she had done something that would get her punished.

He touched her lips with the oily tip of the pizza, until she nibbled off a piece. It was cheese. "That good?" he asked. "I forgot to ask if you had allergies or anything, so I just got this."

She nodded. He kept a tight grip on her arm and watched her intensely as he fed her. "Is this turning you on like it's turning me on?" he asked, bobbing his erection.

"Yes," she said, then continued chewing.

"I'm going to fuck you," he said.

She swallowed. "I know."

He offered her another bite of pizza. She took a big one that time, looking into his eyes as she chewed.

"Keep your hand tight on my dick," he said.

She squeezed him obediently, watching his reaction. He opened his mouth and groaned loudly, throwing his head back. When he looked at her again, there was an intensity she hadn't seen before. He put the slice of pizza back in the box, rubbed his hands on his jeans, sat in the chair and told Autumn to take off his boots.

A pleasant chill went up her spine at the sound of the order. "Move for a sec," he said when they were off. She scooted out of the way, watching as he took off his jacket, and then his shirt, exposing a slim, wiry frame with very little body hair.

He was beautiful.

He watched her with a smirk as he removed his jeans, then pulled her onto the bed and lay his nude body on top of hers. "Tonight, you're mine," he said. "No matter what anyone else's plans are."

He kissed her forcefully while his hand roamed her body, squeezing her breast, playing its fingertips over her stomach and down to her hip. He squeezed her thigh and rear, absently running his thumb over the pulse in her groin, pressing into it, pushing at her with his hips when he found it.

Finally, he came up for air and looked down as he took his erection in his hand. His face drew her eyes, and she knew this was a man who could own her very easily. With a couple of quick pumps of his hips, he was inside her, propping on his elbows and looking down at her curiously.

"You may want to get away from Claudio, but you still like a man who takes charge. If he doesn't let Adam have you and I wind up with you, I may consider putting you over my knee on his behalf. Sort of a lesson about what will happen if you weren't nice and obedient in my house."

Autumn felt a pinching sensation as both nipples suddenly went very erect. She hadn't expected him to say that and wondered if he was serious. Gooseflesh erupted up and down her arms and along her back.

"You don't believe me? You'd better. In fact, I may just give you a little demonstration when I'm done fucking you," he said sternly, thrusting harder. His eyes left hers only long enough for him to locate her wrists and push them into the mattress. He pressed his lips together and held her gaze, pounding the length of his erection into her over and over again.

When he finished, he rolled off and stared at the ceiling. "I would really like a taste of you," he said, raising up on his elbow to look at her. "You know that. You smell fucking awesome and you feel very good around my cock."

In spite of how wild the past few days had been, she blushed. "Everybody says that," she said. "It's like you vampires have some…charm thing or something. Y'all always know the right thing to say to make a girl feel beautiful."

"You think that Manny guy back there could make anyone feel beautiful?"

"Well, maybe not him," she said.

"It helps to be able to get along with people. But have you considered that, if so many men are telling you you're beautiful, that you might just *be* beautiful?"

"That's the nicest thing—"

"It's not a 'nice thing.' It's true. You're fucking gorgeous. Claudio du Fresne prides himself on being a connoisseur. And I know what's hot when I see it myself. And you are smokin'."

She smiled and dropped her gaze.

"Now," he said. "About that demonstration."

Autumn looked up at him, suddenly alarmed.

"It'll have to wait until tomorrow, because all I want to do right now is hold your body next to mine until I get horny again, and then I'm going to have my way with you over, and over, and over..."

Chapter Eighteen

MALCOLM MADE good on his word, rolling Autumn over on her stomach while she was still sleeping and fucking her from behind until they both dropped back off from exhaustion. The next morning, she crept out of bed and looked out the window, remembering Francois. The thought of him sent unpleasant shivers all over her body. Things could have ended up very badly. She felt happy to be safe with Malcolm and on her way back to Claudio and Adam.

Adam. She hadn't known she would miss him so much. At the same time, he wasn't exactly a take-charge kind of guy.

Not that it mattered. It looked like Claudio would be the one to choose who she would be with. Trying not to wonder just how much trouble she was in, she sat down in the chair by the table and tried to open the pizza box quietly. She had gotten nearly all the way through a slice by the time she realized Malcolm had raised up on his elbow and was watching her.

She inhaled suddenly and went into a coughing fit.

He laughed and got up, his nude body moving gracefully toward the bathroom. He was already hard. "Finish that up," he said. "It's time for your demonstration."

"Of what?" she asked.

"I told you last night you were going over my knee first thing this morning," he said with a sly smile and closed the door.

"You did?" she asked.

When he came back out, he wriggled into his jeans and shooed her out of the chair. While she looked on with ever-widening eyes, nibbling on a piece of pizza crust, he moved the chair to the foot of the bed and sat in it, then patted his thighs with both hands.

"Come on."

"But…"

He shook his head. "If I have to come get you, it's going to be much worse," he said. "Now, come over here."

Confused and teary-eyed, she put down her crust and went to him. "I didn't do anything," she said.

"I think you've done a lot of things over the past few days," he said, taking her over his knee. "Like putting yourself in a lot of danger, and making the people who care about you worry. I wouldn't call that nothing."

He rubbed his hand over the round cheek of her bottom. It would have felt good if she didn't know what was coming. It had been a while since she had been punished for real. She began to tear up again.

"You were lucky this time. But there still have to be consequences," he said, bringing his hand down hard on her rear, repeatedly and quickly. It wasn't long before she was squirming against his thighs and whimpering with the pain of the spanking.

"Oh, are you starting to feel a little regretful?" he asked.

Autumn nodded.

Malcolm smacked her ass again, hard. "I can't *hear* you."

"Yes, sir."

"Good," he said. "Here. Get up."

She stood, but wasn't quite sure what to do next, except wipe a stray tear from her eye. "Aww," he said. "I made it cry." He took her on his lap and held her tightly against him. "If you were mine, and you ran away like that, I can't promise you there wouldn't be a belt involved somehow."

That made her think of Claudio, and thinking of Claudio made her tear up even more.

"Shh..." Malcolm said. "It's over now."

"Claudio's going to punish me," she whined.

"Maybe not," he said. "I'll tell him I gave you a pretty decent spanking. Probably not what you deserve, but you've had a pretty hard night. And Manny got you pretty good with that belt."

"You vampires love belts."

"They're efficient," he said, guiding her off his lap and standing up. "And they're convenient. Eat some more if you want to and come back to bed. We didn't get much sleep last night. Plus, I'm horny again."

Chapter Nineteen

A FEW hours later, Malcolm led Autumn to the door of the room she shared with Adam and Maria at Biali House. Hearing Claudio's voice inside, she stopped.

"I can't," she said.

Malcolm shook his head. "Don't make me do this," he said.

Claudio flung open the door and stood there, nostrils flaring. "Is she all right?"

Malcolm caught her arm and hitched it up high, then tugged her forward. "A little worse for wear, but not too bad."

Claudio motioned with his head. "Bring her in."

"Hey, Claudio," Malcolm said in a low voice. "I spanked her this morning for the whole thing."

"Why?"

"As a lesson, in case." He looked around. "Hey, look. I like her. If you decide you don't want her and you don't want Adam to have her, well..." He shrugged.

"I'll consider it," Claudio said, giving Autumn a look that nearly froze her to the spot, before returning to the room. She looked away.

She did not follow on her own, but had to be tugged by Malcolm. "Come on," he ordered. "You're just making it harder on yourself by stalling."

"But..."

"Don't make me tell you again," he said.

Inside, Maria sprang from the bed toward Autumn, smiling and crying, but Claudio put up his arm to stop her. Maria's smile faded as she shifted on her feet and looked from Claudio to Malcolm to Autumn.

Adam, who had been leaning against the dresser with his arms crossed over his chest and his head down, looked up and was halfway to Autumn before Claudio could put his hand on Adam's shoulder. Adam stopped and looked at it.

"Business first," Claudio said.

Adam scowled. "Get off me. The girl has been through I don't know what. I want to make sure she's okay."

The two men locked eyes for a moment. Claudio tightened his jaw, put his left hand on his hip, and took his hand off Adam's shoulder to flourish violently with it. Then he turned away.

Adam turned to Malcolm. "What did you do to her?"

"Nothing she didn't want," Malcolm said. His eyes never wavered. "I got her out of there."

Adam nodded. "Thanks," he said, then took Autumn off her feet in a bear hug. "Oh my God, baby girl. Oh my God. What did that punk-ass motherfucker Francois do to you?"

Autumn felt so relieved, the only thing she could do in response was cry and tremble against him. She felt another hand on her hair and turned to see it was Maria, who had ventured over when Claudio turned away. Malcolm moved toward Claudio as they embraced her. Finally, Autumn was able to speak.

"What's happening?"

"Claudio is deciding what to do about you and Maria," Adam said.

Autumn began to cry again. She put her hand over her mouth and shut her eyes tight.

"Maria," Claudio said sharply. "Autumn. Come. Sit." He motioned with his hand toward the foot of the bed.

Autumn looked up at Adam, reluctant to leave his embrace, but the urgency in Claudio's voice made her pull away. A few days ago, she had actually believed she would never have to worry about trembling before Claudio again. She sat so close to Maria that the entire length of her thigh pressed against the entire length of the other girl's. Maria was trembling too.

Claudio separated them. "You there, and you…there," he said, pointing to the corners of the mattress. The girls glanced at each other and moved apart. Claudio stood in front of them. Autumn stared at his shoes. They had a high polish, as always. He was always so immaculately dressed. It was one of the things that had attracted her to him in the beginning. She clasped her hands and pressed them into her lap, resisting the urge to rock for comfort.

"Autumn," he said. His French accent seemed stronger than she remembered.

"Yes, sir?"

"Do you know what is happening here?"

She nodded. "You're trying to decide what to do with me and Maria."

"I'm trying to decide what is *best* for you and Maria. But first, I would like to know why you felt it was necessary to leave, yes?"

Maria sat up straight. "We—"

"From her," Claudio said. "I want to hear Autumn's reasons, not yours. Yours, I know."

Maria looked around the room sheepishly, then wilted.

Claudio smiled at Autumn. "Tell me, *cherie*," he said gently. "Why you want to leave my home."

"I wanted…I wanted to be with Maria."

She heard the other girl take in a breath, and from the corner of her eye saw Maria's hand go to her mouth.

"And now?"

Autumn shook her head. "I thought I was in love, but I just…I love her as a friend." She hated the way the words sounded. Knew how horrible they must sound to Maria, how the attempt at kindness probably hurt just as much as outright cruelty. But she couldn't bring herself to be cruel to Maria, not even to make things easier later on.

"What changed your mind?" Claudio asked.

"Freedom," Autumn said without hesitating. "I wanted to experience things on my own terms." Again, she winced at her words. They sounded like something a TV character would say.

"Yes," Claudio said. "Freedom can be a potent drug. What did you find while you were free?"

Autumn looked at him, unsure what he meant. Her heart raced. She knew he liked to have answers when he asked questions, but she didn't have one. "I don't…" she began. "I don't understand."

"What have you been doing, besides getting yourself kidnapped?"

She hung her head, blushing.

"Maria?" he said suddenly.

Maria's head snapped up. "Yes, sir?"

"What has Autumn been doing with this freedom of hers?"

Maria looked at Autumn.

"Give me the truth," Claudio said. "I am basing my decision on what she needs. Nothing more."

Maria took a deep breath. "She's…been exploring…"

"She's been fucking around," Malcolm said from across the room. He leaned against the wall at the head of the bed with his arms and ankles crossed. He walked to Claudio without looking at Autumn. "She told me. It's been one guy after another, ending with me. What this little girl needs is a firm hand on her backside. She doesn't need to be allowed to run wild, because what she looks for is somebody to make her behave. I think she's just been shopping for a new master."

Autumn couldn't believe what she was hearing. When Claudio looked at her, she looked away with burning cheeks.

"Is this true?" he asked.

"I…I don't know."

"I can tell you how she reacted to what I did," Malcolm said, "which was to tell her how I discipline my girls when they need it, and to make her give me what I wanted. She mewled like a kitten."

Claudio turned his attention back to her. "This is what you had at my home, Autumn. Do you wish to return?"

She shook her head vigorously, eyes tearing up and voice cracking. "No. I don't want to go back."

"Why, *cherie*?"

"Because it's too much. You're too much. I'm afraid all the time. I can't please you. Even being in the room with you like this, it's…" Her voice hitched in her throat and she began to sob.

Some of the sternness left Claudio's face. He fluttered his eyes and gave her a forced smile, then nodded. "I see. Knowing you as I do, I believe what Malcolm says is true, that you need to belong to a vampire. Perhaps I am the wrong one, but I also do not believe Adam is the right one."

"Why not?" Autumn asked, suddenly panicking, realizing that, even as she strayed, she had counted on Adam's presence to anchor her. Without that, she didn't know what she would do.

"You want to be with Adam?" Claudio asked.

Autumn nodded.

"Why?"

"Because I love him."

"But Adam cannot give you what you need, *cherie*. You need direction, guidance. Discipline. He and I have spoken about this subject many times. He is not the one."

Malcolm puffed out his chest.

Adam moved closer. "Now wait a minute. That's what the two of you say. You're both trying to justify the way you do things by saying it's what they want. Like happy little slaves just thrilled to take a beating for massa's pleasure."

"Adam—" Claudio began.

"No. You are going to have to convince me this is what's good for her. And then we can talk about whether I'm the right vampire to take her."

"Very well," Claudio said. "Malcolm, it sounds like you had some success with her. Why don't you give Adam a little demonstration? Show us how she reacts to someone like you, yes?"

Chapter Twenty

AUTUMN LOOKED nervously up at Malcolm, wondering what he was going to do. He got her attention by approaching her deliberately and standing to her side, feet apart, staring. "Autumn," he said firmly.

She straightened her posture and widened her eyes.

He waited.

She looked around the room, first at Adam, then over her shoulder at Claudio.

"Autumn," Malcolm repeated. "I'm speaking to you."

She snapped her head around to look at him, uncertain what was expected of her. She shivered. "Yes sir?"

"Do you remember your spanking this morning?" he asked.

Autumn looked down, feeling her cheeks redden, and the spot between her legs grow warm. "Yes, sir."

"How did it make you feel?"

She shook her head. "I…I can't…"

"Yes, you can," he said, taking a step toward her. "How did it make you feel?"

"Afraid," she said.

"Is that all?"

She shook her head. "Ashamed, and…"

"And what? Either tell me or say there is nothing else, or you will get another one right here and right now."

"Excited," she said, nodding. "It made me excited."

Adam uncrossed his arms. "This is bullshit. You know and I know this girl will say or do anything a man wants for approval. She knows he wants to hear this stuff."

Claudio put up his hand.

Malcolm continued. "You remember what it was like to be spanked by me, don't you? When I pulled you across my knee and started teaching you a little lesson?"

She nodded.

"Now I want you to do something for me, okay? I want you to pull down your jeans and your underwear and show Adam just how wet you are."

Adam threw up his hands. "This is in—"

"He is right," Claudio said. "This is a very good way to tell. Autumn."

She looked at Claudio for a moment, wondering if there was any way out of this. Seeing none, she kicked off her shoes, then stood and pulled off her pants, reasoning she looked less silly with them gone than with them down. She stood with her hands clasped in front of her and her head down, feeling her cheeks burn.

"Adam," Claudio said.

Adam sighed and bulled across the room, controlling his movements only upon reaching Autumn. "Let me check you, baby girl, okay?" he said, rubbing her stomach with the backs of his fingers and looking into her eye.

She nodded.

He reached between her legs and slid a finger in easily. She was so wet, her juices trickled over the labia and onto his hand. "Damn, girl," he said. "Is he telling the truth? Do you really need someone to do that?"

"I guess so," she said softly.

Autumn wondered if Adam was simply too gentle to give her what she needed, and if that fact sentenced her to a life with Claudio or with this stranger. It was out of her control.

"Autumn," Claudio said. "If you wish to return with me, there is a place for you. What is your decision?"

Her heart beat ferociously as she looked at him. Miraculously, she shook her head. "I don't want to go back," she said barely above a whisper.

Claudio pursed his lips. "Very well," he said. "I would have chosen, then, for you to remain with Adam. But I think you will not obey a vampire who is afraid to discipline you. Therefore—"

"Wait a minute," Adam said, quickly. "I can learn. If that's what she really needs, I can learn to do it."

Claudio regarded him with an amused smile. "You can learn to punish her?"

Adam nodded. "Yeah. If she needs it. I can do that." He looked around. "Look, she needs to be with someone she knows. No offense, man," she said to Malcolm, "but I just don't think going into somebody else's situation is going to do her much good right now. Maybe later, but not right now."

Claudio nodded slowly. "I know this man. He has a firm hand, but he is fair. With a slave like this one, it is very important to have someone who understands these things. However, if you can convince me, Adam, that you are able to control her in the way she needs to be controlled, you may have her."

Autumn saw Adam bristle at the word "slave," but she thought something about it rang true. She *was* a slave—to this lifestyle, to any man who knew how to use the tingle of fear to make her behave. She had thought her desire to leave Claudio's estate meant she had outgrown it, but now she knew that wasn't true. She needed the security of being told what to do.

"Do you think you can do that, Adam?"

Adam sighed, rubbed the top of his head, and looked around at the other men. "If that's what she needs, then I can do it."

"It is always what they need, Adam. There is a reason they want to belong to us."

Adam nodded. "Right. Sure. I can do it."

"Good," Claudio said, then motioned with his hand toward Autumn.

Adam pulled his head back and widened his eyes. "What? You mean now?"

"Now is the perfect time. She has been disobedient. Did you give her permission to encourage Francois?"

"No, but…"

"Then make sure she understands it is not acceptable."

Adam rolled his eyes, sighed, and turned around one of the straight-backed chairs. Sitting, he put his hands on his thighs and pressed his lips together. Autumn thought he looked very uncomfortable. With one final glance at Claudio, Adam took a deep breath and turned his eyes on Autumn. There was no way he was going to do this, she thought. He couldn't. He wouldn't be Adam anymore.

"Get over here," he said. His voice wasn't exactly harsh, but it did sound strained.

Autumn looked at Maria, who gave her a sad smile and nodded. It was good to know her best friend didn't hate her for not being able to be her lover anymore.

Autumn stepped forward. Adam watched.

When she stood near him, Claudio said, "Take her into position, Adam. You must do this. Sometimes, they will even resist. You are the one who must make it happen."

Adam nodded and sighed, then took Autumn's arm and pulled her awkwardly over his lap. She couldn't help but resist at least a little, leaning back against his grip at the last moment. She remembered the spanking Malcolm had given her. It had been short, but painful. She wasn't sure whether she wanted to think of Adam this way.

"Wait!" she cried out, struggling to push herself up. "I have to get up for a second."

She felt Adam hesitate. Then his body tensed and he said, "No. You should have thought of that before."

She yelped when he brought his hand down the first time. He did it only hard enough to sting, but being spanked by Adam was strange.

"Harder," Claudio said. "This is punishment. It is not supposed to be pleasant."

Again, Adam hesitated. Again, he took a deep breath. Autumn waited. Then he began delivering a series of painful blows to her backside that made her squirm. "Adam!" she called desperately, but he didn't stop. Instead, he used his free arm to hold her down while he made her bottom warm with his other hand.

Finally, she stopped struggling against his grip or fighting her tears. She grew still and let them come. It had been a long time since she'd had the luxury of crying and now tears seemed to tumble out effortlessly.

He seemed to know when she'd had enough, when her body just wasn't able to take anymore, and he stopped.

For a moment, she didn't move. Autumn had been spanked before—by Claudio, by the musician she'd met at Jean Lafitte's, and by Malcolm—but this one had affected her more than any of the others, and she couldn't quite move.

Claudio spoke softly. "You have to bring them back. Sometimes they forget to move."

Adam rubbed her back. "Time to get up," he said gently.

She tried to scramble off his lap, but he had to help her. She swayed on her feet. Something moved behind her, but it was only Malcolm handing her the jeans and panties he had bought for her. She took them gratefully and put them on.

No sooner had she zipped and buttoned them, than she became aware that Claudio was moving slowly toward her. His presence still made her tremble. "Such a delicate thing," he said, reaching to move the hair out of the way and caress the sensitive flesh of her neck. "Have you learned your lesson?"

Autumn nodded and began to cry again. She covered her face with her hands as the sobs made her shoulders convulse. Adam was up in a shot, and put his arms around her, squeezing her to his chest. Autumn peeked at Claudio for a moment, to find him watching with interest.

"It's all right," Adam whispered. "It's okay. But you can't run off and do things like that anymore."

She shut her eyes tight and nodded. Her bottom hurt, a lot, but Adam's arms were warm around her. For the first time in a very long time, she realized, she felt safe.

"Very interesting," Claudio said. "Perhaps there is a chance for you, yes?"

Chapter Twenty-One

OVER THE next week, both Claudio and Malcolm—and occasionally Freddie and Mick—coached Adam on the training and discipline of feeders. Autumn enjoyed the attention, and couldn't move quickly enough when one of the men wanted her to pour a cocktail. She desperately wanted to be bitten, but they all thought it best that she take a few days off, after having been so drained by Francois.

She worried about Maria. Claudio had decided to take her back to the estate with him, and Autumn knew that meant a terrible whipping, possibly in front of Claudio's other feeders. Maria, who had always had a handy quip or snicker, sat quietly watching as the men worked with Autumn. Her eyes seemed to light up only when Autumn looked at her, and that made Autumn's heart ache.

She almost wished she wasn't taking to the attention so readily. In fact, it hardly seemed Autumn needed training at all. It was Adam's name that Claudio said most often, instructing him to ask for things, and to constantly remind Autumn of his position over her.

"Why do I have to do that?" Adam asked after a couple of days. "She's a smart girl. She knows."

Malcolm was the one to answer. "They like to be reminded, that's why," he said. "It's like foreplay for them. Every time you speak to her a certain way, it's like you're stroking her with your voice. I'll bet you could keep this one wet for you all the time by doing that."

Adam hung his head and smiled. "That could be a good thing."

Autumn happened to be looking at him when he turned to her. She blushed. *Yeah,* she thought, *safe,* but…

But now, there was new possibility in that safety. When he told her to come to him, there was an edge to his voice. Autumn soon found she liked to test it, just to see if he really was getting what Claudio and Malcolm were telling him.

She was certainly getting it. Now that she knew Claudio would no longer be taking her or punishing her, he didn't seem quite as scary, and the sound of his voice sent pleasant shivers up her spine like it had when they had first met.

She felt a little bad for Malcolm, but she didn't want to leave Adam.

At the end of the week, Malcolm left them to return to his home and his feeders, and Claudio took Adam and Autumn to Austin, Texas, where he knew of a vampire co-op that would help them get on their feet. Within a day, Adam had a job as a bartender at a local bar and weekly music gigs there.

The next day, the four of them stood on the front porch, saying their goodbyes. Maria waited slightly behind Claudio while Autumn hugged Adam's arm.

"You will not live as well here," Claudio said, shaking his head.

"But I'll be living free," Adam answered.

"We will keep in touch," Claudio said. "I will not abandon my family."

Adam nodded as they shook hands. "I appreciate it. I really do. I appreciate everything you've ever done for me, Claudio. I mean that. I don't want you to think that's not true."

Claudio bowed his head with a smile, then leaned forward to place a kiss on Autumn's forehead. "Take care, *cherie*," he said.

She smiled. "Yes, sir."

Then she turned to Maria, who hugged her silently and hard before turning away and hurrying to Claudio's car. Her sudden departure brought tears to Autumn's eyes, but she knew they'd be in touch. She'd e-mail Maria tomorrow to see how she was doing.

She and Adam stood there for several moments, watching them go.

"Well," he said finally, putting his arm around her shoulders. "This is it."

"Yeah," she said, casting a sideways glance at him and putting hair behind her ear bashfully. "I guess it is."

"You know what? I think I'm hungry. And you *know* what that means."

Butterflies fluttered in Autumn's belly at his suggestive tone, but instead of making her acquiesce immediately, it filled her with mischief, and she ducked out from under his arm.

He raised his eyebrows at her. She stood there, with the tip of her thumb in her mouth, looking at him over her shoulder.

"Girl, you better stop playing," he said.

She turned and faced him, swinging her arms and walking backward. Grinning.

He hung his head and grinned back, showing his extended fangs. "You're gonna make me chase—"

Before the words were out of his mouth, Autumn had turned, flung open the screen door and run inside.

The house was a sprawling mess of a floor-plan, with three wings of bedrooms and hallways bookending the kitchen and main living space. Adam and Autumn shared a room in the most isolated, quiet hallway of the house, where the more studious tenants tended to live. Autumn ran loudly down the hallway, losing a flip-flop and doubling back for it, all arms and legs. Her hand shook excitedly as she fumbled with the key to their room but, before she knew it, Adam was behind her, pressing her into the door.

"So you want to play like this, little girl?" he asked, breathing on the back of her neck, bending down and nipping the place where shoulder joins neck, ever so lightly.

She let her mouth fall open and her eyelids droop. A bolt of excitement—the sort of deep-down excitement that went clear to the bone—ripped through her. She had never felt that way with Adam before. Unable to move, she waited.

"You want this big, black cock in you?" he asked.

Her breath hitched.

"Hmm?" he asked, letting his voice sound insistent, pressing her into the door with his hips, letting her feel the hardened shaft of his erection against her backside.

She nodded.

"Open the door," he rasped, and stepped away.

By now, her hands shook so much, it took her several seconds to get the key in the lock. Once inside the tiny space, she put the key on the corner of the desk by the door and hurried to open the window. There were house rules against it, because of the air conditioner, but it was much too hot to leave it shut. A gust of air blew the long strands of hair around her face. She breathed it in, listening to the sound of the door closing and locking behind her.

She waited a moment, enjoying the feel of her heart pounding from running, from anticipation. Then she turned around.

Adam was looking at her. He shrugged. "Take off your clothes," he said.

She did, and stood naked before him.

"Lie down and play with yourself."

She turned to make sure she knew where the futon was and positioned herself on it so that he could see her newly shaved crotch, then opened her legs wide and dipped her fingers into her own juices. She was very wet.

The air played over her nude body, teasing her nipples to points.

Adam pulled his T-shirt over his head and grinned. "Huh. I could get used to this. You'll do anything I tell you, won't you?" he said.

She grinned, and nodded as he climbed on top of her.

"Well then, fix me some lunch," he said.

She threw her head back to expose her throat for him. Her heart raced as she thought of his fangs piercing the skin and felt his erection press against her thigh. He slid his arms under her and held her tightly as he probed her throat with the tip of his tongue. Autumn became very still, hardly daring to breathe as she waited for the tingling prick of the fangs pushing into her skin and the subsequent mellow euphoria that came with a deep feeding.

He fucked her while he fed, using his hand to guide his meaty cock into her, filling and stretching her, piercing the flesh, thrusting and sucking, until she lost track of where his hypnotic undulations ended and her responses began. His weight and his breathing comforted her. She hid among his ropey dreads and took in his musk, drifting, aware only of sensation.

When it was over, she lay half under him as he held her loosely. "That was good," he said, and yawned. "I might have to have some more later."

"Okay," she said, and breathed him deeply.

This is it, she thought, feeling as though she had been waiting for this moment for a long time, a temporary rest with a man she could feel safe with, but who could make her hot with anticipation at a moment's notice. Someone who would tell her what he wanted, and provide consequences if it wasn't done. Not harsh consequences, but just a little reminder.

Over the past week, Adam had begun to understand that need, and had discovered he was becoming capable of providing for it. Autumn couldn't explain why, but just knowing that made her feel safe.

She lay with his arm and leg thrown over her body, and his hip resting against the side of hers, feeling him breathe, smelling the scents of his musk mixed with essential oils, and the incense he loved to burn.

As if the earth and the trees and the sky could hear her thoughts, a stronger gust of air blew in through the window. She angled her face upward and let it kiss her, shivering pleasantly as it tickled over her skin. Adam shifted, smiled and sighed softly.

THE END

Also Available from Red Silk Editions

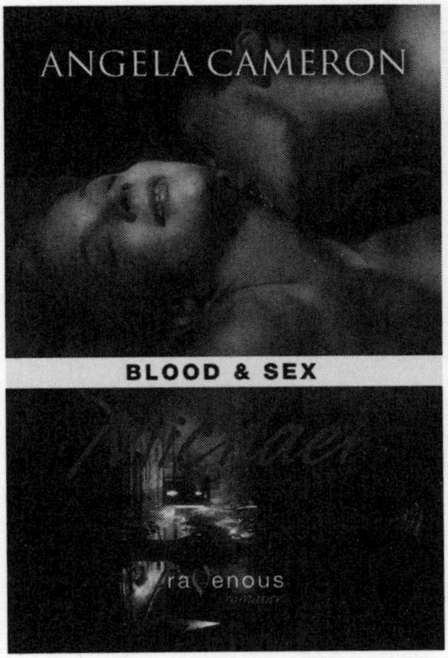

Blood & Sex: Michael
by Angela Cameron

This is a spine-chilling and erotic tale of a Mafia vampire and the detective who is determined to bring to justice a serial killer. Detective Victoria Tyler allows Mafia vampire Michael to "take her neck" and lead her on a journey through a world of bondage, domination, and blood to stop the killer. But can she resist the dark lusts he sparks?

Volume 1 in the Blood & Sex series

Paperback: $12.95

978-1-59003-203-9

Available in August 2010

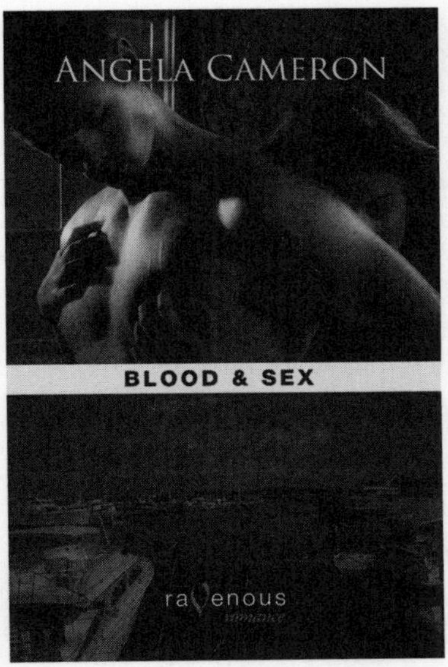

Blood & Sex: Jonas
by Angela Cameron

Jonas, the strangely appealing owner of the new vampire-themed bondage club could be the perfect distraction for workaholic Dr. Elena Jensen. But their worlds couldn't be farther apart....

Volume 2 of the Blood & Sex series

Paperback: $12.95

978-1-59003-202-2

Available in October 2010

Blood & Sex: Blane
by Angela Cameron

Will Blane be able to break through the guarded reserve of Christiana, the beautiful woman the vampire leader has sent to educate the newest vampires? Or will her sense of duty be stronger than the passion that threatens to sweep her away?

Volume 3 of the Blood & Sex series

Paperback: $12.95

978-1-59003-206-0

Available in December 2010

The Maestro's Butterfly
by Rhonda Leigh Jones

Miranda O'Connell has just made a dangerous bet with her mysterious, sexy music teacher that will change her life forever. Will she fall in love with the kinky vampire Maestro and submit to life as a feeder slave? Or will she escape the confines of his estate for the dashing, dangerous charms of his brother?

Paperback: $12.95

978-1-59003-207-7

Available in November 2010

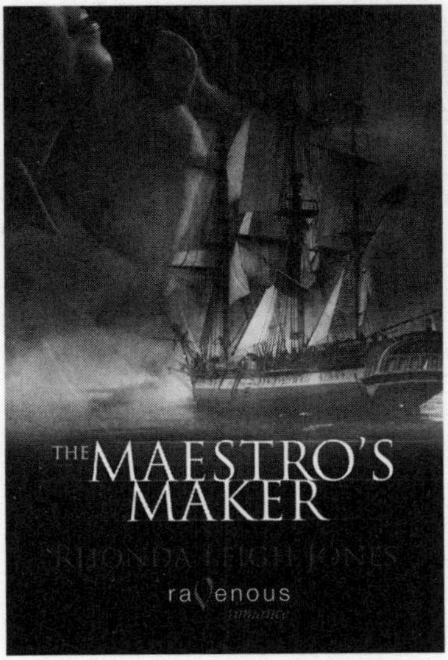

The Maestro's Maker
by Rhonda Leigh Jones

Trapped between two vampires: Chloe discovers the darkness that binds the beautiful and arrogant French noble Claudio du Fresne and his oldest friend Francois Villaforte. With danger, intrigue, and kinky sex, *The Maestro's Maker* takes vampire erotica to passionate new levels!

Paperback: $12.95

978-1-59003-210-7

Available in December 2010

The Maestro's Apprentice
by Rhonda Leigh Jones

For the first time in her life, Autumn is free. She has escaped Claudio du Fresne, the vampire for whom she had been a feeder-slave for years. Now she wants to play, and for her, playing means wild, crazy sex with strangers.

Paperback: $12.95

978-1-59003-209-1

Available in January 2011

The Dark Desires of the Druids: Sex & Subterfuge by Isabel Roman

"Do you like jealous heroes and love triangles? How about sizzling sexual encounters atop dining room furniture? If you answered yes to either question, you're going to love this novella." —Susan S., loveromance.passion.com

Paperback: $12.95

978-1-59003-200-8

Available in August 2010

The Dark Desires of the Druids: Desert and Destiny by Isabel Roman

The first time they met, Arbelle Bahari tried to kill him. The second time, they made love on a desk in the British Museum.

"The action is fast and exciting, the mystery is engaging, and the romance is searingly hot." —*Whipped Cream Reviews* (5 Cherries)

Paperback: $12.95

978-1-59003-201-5

Available in October 2010

Bites of Passion
edited by Cecilia Tan

What does it mean to love a vampire? Does it mean nights of pleasure tempered with sweet pain? Eight top authors explore the themes of immortal love, the lust for blood, and the eternal struggle between light and dark.

Paperback: $12.95

978-1-59003-205-3

Available in September 2010

Magic University: The Siren and the Sword
by Cecilia Tan

Harvard freshman Kyle Wadsorth is eager to start a new life. Surprises abound when he discovers a secret magical university hidden inside Harvard and he meets Jess Torralva, who tutors him in the ways of magic, sex, and love.

Paperback: $12.95

978-1-59003-208-4

Available in November 2010

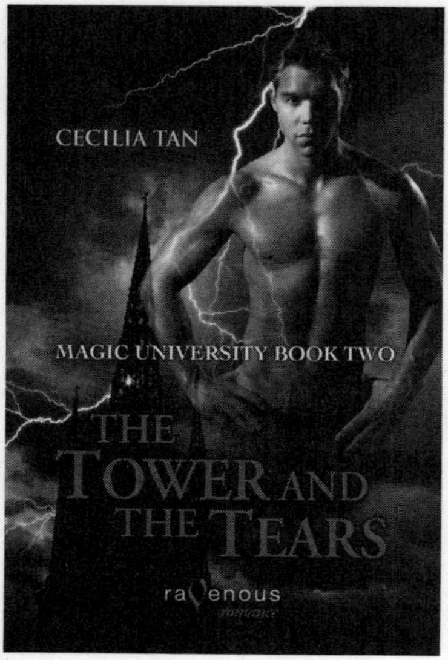

Magic University: The Tower and the Tears by Cecilia Tan

This second volume in the Magic University series brings together myth, magic, and eroticism for adult readers of fantasy who want a bedtime tale of their own.

"Simply one of the most important writers, editors, and innovators in contemporary American erotic literature."—Susie Bright

Paperback: $12.95

978-1-59003-211-4

Available in January 2011

Mind Games by Cecilia Tan

Who hasn't fantasized about using psychic abilities to satisfy your every sexual desire? *Mind Games* provides readers the opportunity to live out that dream....

"Scorching hot with a touch of suspense. Cecilia Tan brings together love, suspense, and scorching sex in a story well worth reading."—*ParaNormal Romance Review*

Paperback: $12.95

978-1-59003-204-6

Available in September 2010

Notes

Notes

Notes

Notes